Volume Two
Mystery Mountain
More Adventures Of A Mountain Family and Community
Marie Grace

Author of
The Mystery Mountain Collection
Volumes One, Two, Three and Four,
Thoughts Aplenty

Mystery Mountain, Volume Two
More Adventures of a Mountain Family and Community
Marie Grace
Author of The Mystery Mountain Collection: Volumes One, Two, Three and
Four; and, Thoughts Aplenty

Copyright © Marie Grace

Published By Parables
February, 2018

Unless otherwise specified Scripture quotations are taken from the authorized version of the King James Bible.

ISBN 978-1-945698-48-4
Printed in the United States of America

Readers should be aware that Internet Web sites offered as citations and/or sources for further information may have been changed or disappeared between the time this was written and when it is read.

Volume Two

Mystery Mountain

More Adventures Of A Mountain Family and Community

Marie Grace

Author of
The Mystery Mountain Collection
Volumes One, Two, Three and Four,
Thoughts Aplenty

MYSTERY MOUNTAIN TWO

Dedication

It is my honor to dedicate this second book in my Mystery Mountain Series to Dr. John Dee Jeffries.

Dr. Jeffries is the Founder, CEO and Acquisitions Editor of Published by Parables. He is a proven 'Man of God' by his 40 plus years as a pastor, teacher, and author. Dr. Jeffries has authored many books, including The Last Martyr, To The Shepherds, When I Can't Find God, and Hip Hip Hallelujah, plus many others. He is the Senior Pastor of First Baptist Church in Chalmette, Lousiana, where he and his wife, Genny, have served the Lord and others for over 25 years.

Being an Author and Publisher he is very aware of the hoops so many authors have to jump through to get their work published. He is a good, solid 'helper' and adviser.

Dr. Jeffries was ordained April 2, 1978, on his 30th birthday. He and Genny have been serving God's churches ever since. They met in high school and attended Bible college and Seminary together. People who know this godly man, Dr. Jeffries, say he is an Evangelist, whose heart is geared to making disciples of others, and pointing them to Jesus Christ. He has served as the Senior Pastor at four churches, and has led thousands to the saving knowledge of Jesus Christ.

He and Genny are big time missions promoters. He was even sponsoring NINE missions churches at the same time. (I sometimes wonder if he ever sleeps.)

When hurricane Katrina devastated their community, every house, building, church and school were flooded or completely destroyed. Dr. Jeffries led the horrendous task of raising roughly $4.1 million dollars to help victims, and to rebuild their own campus and sanctuary. He also mobilized 4,500 volunteers to help all the building projects in the area. (As I said, I wonder if he ever sleeps.)

On top of everything else, he launched many critical ministries to the Community; a food pantry that distributes roughtly 20,000 pounds of food each month to the needy and homeless. He introduced many traditional and contemporary ministries; a bicycle ministry, a day care, a counseling and teaching, etc..

One of his favorite sayings is: "Still running the race for Christ."

Are you still running the race for Christ? There will always be bumps and caverns along the way, but as Paul tells us, Phillipians 3:14, "We must press on toward the mark for the prize of the high calling of God in Jesus Christ." Dr. John Dee Jeffries is the example of someone it is safe to follow in the path toward Christ Jesus.

If you have a Christian based book you think will help others along this sometimes rough road in earth, and will help build confidence in Christ, Published by Parables will publish it free, if accepted, you may contact them at www.publishedbyparables.com. The amazing CEO/Acquisitions Editor Dr. John Dee Jeffries, will help you with your walk into the ministry of Books.

Thank you, Pastor Jeffries.
Marie Grace

Table of Contents

Introduction

Mystery Mountain (Two) starts where *Mystery Mountain (One)* left off. A federal officer orders Jake and Ira back down into the dangerous canyon - to catch two killers. The federal officer just happens to be a lady - who insists on accompanying them.

The hero lady wolf that rescued the little girl is now facing certain death.

With Jake's arm in a cast descending three hundred feet down into the canyon is an unbelievable task.

When Jake's secret project nears the end, he asks his love to be his wife in one of the most romantic proposals ever.

As the love story continues, other love stories come into focus. Two young men suffer the lingering effects of Sickle Cell Anemia. A powerful blacksmith may have his dream come true by God giving him a family to care for.

Young love sprouts as an Exchange comes to Raincroft. Dancing and music fills the whole town. Six roughian boys learn right from wrong - the hard way, mountain style, in the Sheriff's jail. A young deputy becomes a man, and a bully is appointed Special Deputy.

Come visit Raincroft again, as the Mountain and Woods People try to carve out an existence amid the harsh surroundings in this deep, moving, and often heartbreaking sequel *Mystery Mountain (Two)*.

All scripture references are from the King James Bible unless otherwise stated.

Wounds & Rabies

Mam was working on cleaning Jake's arm between his bites of homemade stew. Ira was really inhaling the delicious dish; he acted like he hadn't eaten for weeks. With Ira's mother dying at Billy's birth, the rugged man's home cooked meals were scarce.

Jake winced a couple of times and Mam backed off to let him catch his breath. The teeth marks were deep, and they had torn the flesh to the bone. Josie knew he would need stitches.

"Sometimes wild animals have rabies and that is why they attack. You can never be sure when you don't have the animal to check. Other times you are just prey, and it's always good to be safe rather than sorry," Josie was saying, "Doc Lowery will say for sure if he can sew Jake up or if he will have to go into City Hospital when you boys visit him in the morning."

The peroxide fizzed pretty white bubbles as she poured it over the wounds on his face and arms.

"I guess right now, it's a good thing you look like a wooly mammoth," Mam was saying to Jake, "that probably stopped you from getting your face all scratched up. You'll have some scars on this arm; -but you can just wear long sleeves."

"It feels like I have a sticker in my arm," Jake told his mom, "I hope it doesn't last too long, it's really irritating."

The men were informing Mam about the day's experiences, and especially the lady wolf.

"Only God will ever know how the lady wolf got the little girl over to that cave," Jake remarked as he shook his head slightly, "but, you sure were right, Mam, God is still doing miracles. It's a wonderment how Missy landed on the ledge instead of going clear to the canyon floor. And, thanks Mam for yours and Jani's prayers."

"You're welcome son," Josie answered.

As soon as she had finished cleaning up Jake she turned her attention to Ira, who was eating his fourth bowl of stew.

"Let's see your scrapes." Josie told him.

"Awe, I'm all right Mam," Ira replied.

"Don't all right me young man," she demanded, "show me your wounds."

Ira looked at Jake and he nodded affirmative to him as he raised his eyebrows a bit.

Ira held out his right arm. The shirt was torn badly, and it was bloody.

"Tangling with critters usually means wounds, let's peroxide them out." Mam told him.

Ira didn't know how much the peroxide was going to hurt him, but he set his jaw and waited for the pain. Almost nothing happened.

"Sore's fresh," Mam remarked, "cleaning doesn't hurt so much when the wound's fresh."

She could see the look of relief in Ira's eyes.

You know, Josie chuckled to herself, *these big boys can tackle mountain lions, bears, coyotes and treacherous conditions, but they are still little boys in their hearts when they are with mom.*

She gave them each two Aleve for pain.

"Ira," Josie asked, "how long has it been since you've had a Rabies Booster?"

"Never, Mam," he replied firmly, "never had any kind of a vaccination or booster in my life, and I don't like shots."

"Too bad big boy," Mam came back, "you'll be going with Jake to Dr. Lowery's in the morning to get yourself protected."

"I don't have any money." Ira said as he resisted a shot.

"Doesn't matter," she replied, "Jake will pay for it."

That settled it, Ira was in for it.

"By the way, Jake," Mam continued, "you can pick up Stria's and Oreo's boosters while you are there. I had the doc order them about a week ago, and he should have them by now."

"Yes Mam." Jake agreed.

"Now, Ira," Josie started, "I understand you committed a very sacred act with Jake, a Blood Covenant, just like we do with the Lord, only we have to do it physically. You know us mountain folk take blood kinship very seriously."

Although Ira didn't understand exactly what a blood covenant with the Lord is, as Josie was saying the words, he knew it is solemn.

"I'm sure Jake has told you," she continued with her eyes set on Ira, "that we are still his parents, and I'll whipper him if he needs it."

"Amen to that." Jake snickered rubbing his bruised backside from the rod of correction.

Mam flashed her eyes at Jake as she continued, "You are now my physical and spiritual son, and I expect you to behave like a gentleman. Especially with the ladies, or I'll whipper you too."

Ira looked half-amused, and half-fearful of this little woman. But he felt like he had become a part of the family. As Jake rolled his eyes over to the broom in the corner, Ira glanced at it too.

He remembered Jake's warning, "If Mam has the broom in her hands and isn't cleaning – run."

"Now here's what's going to happen, Ira, Doc Lowery will be giving you one shot of something called Rabies Immune Globulin. It will give you immediate protection. But he will also give you five more shots for immunization. The Globulin will be as close as possible to one of your worst wounds, but the first of the next five will be in your shoulder's deltoid muscle. You will get your first shoulder injection tomorrow morning, along with the one in your injury. You both will also get Tetanus shots. Doc Lowery will schedule you to return in three days from the first shot, then in seven and then fourteen days and the final one on the twenty-eighth day following your first one tomorrow morning. You will make all of the shots, right?" Mam instructed him as she poked his shoulder to show him where his deltoid muscle is.

"Yes Mam," Ira quickly agreed; the broom was still in the corner.

"Now Jake, I think you may only need the three Booster doses, but Dr. Lowery may require you to have the full series since you were injured so badly. Ed will tell you in the morning. You will have to make appointments for the second and third shots. I already have you boys scheduled for first thing in the morning," Mam informed them, "I called the doc when I went for the peroxide, and he agreed to see you even though it's Sunday - because you are both heroes."

Ira was stunned at Mam's words; the word hero had never been connected with the name Ira Carson - it felt good.

As soon as Jake had finished eating, he took his dishes to the sink, rinsed them and put them in Mam's new dishwasher. Ira followed suit.

"Now, I'll show you around our home." Jake said to Ira, who didn't have to be asked twice. He was actually in Mystery Mountain.

Ira loves to horse around with Karate, but had never been able to afford lessons. Jake showed him the video on Karate and said they could it watch later. He gave Ira a copy of the leaflet instructions and showed him his exercise corner. Before long Mam could hear —bumps —thuds and slams clear down to the kitchen.

That's gotta hurt your arm Jake Judd. Mam thought to herself.

As the Paramedics were en-route to City Hospital for some critical care, Tom and Alex were in contact with the Emergency Room Doctor, and were getting instructions to start IVs on both Keith and Missy. Although Laura is an M.D., Tom didn't feel it was appropriate for her to be issuing orders, especially for her own family. Plus he wanted to be sure the hospital would be waiting for them when they arrived since Keith's blood loss had been pretty severe.

Keith and Laura were both holding Missy's little hand for comfort and security.

Missy was trying to talk softly. "Mommy and Daddy," came out pretty clear, but most of her other words could not be understood. However, Missy said pretty intelligibly, "Muffy; Doggie." They were sure the little girl was talking about the lady wolf that had apparently saved her life. She drifted off to sleep.

"Perhaps when she can talk better she will be able to tell us more of what happened." Laura commented.

"Laura, you should have witnessed those two mountain men doing 'their thing'. I know now where the term 'bear hug' comes from; it's what Jake did to a bear, with a bad arm. I think usually it's the other way around. It was amazing." Keith was filling in his daughter's new mother. "I don't know how much Missy could see from her cave. Did she see the dead mountain lion, or Jake carry the bear off – or the coyotes being shot…or Muffy being shaken…" The medicine in the IV was making Keith groggy, and he was mumbling. "I really do love you Laura…" He said as he drifted off to sleep.

Laura leaned over and kissed his lips softly.

After all the searchers had returned and Sheriff Leo thanked and dismissed everyone, Jess walked Beth up to John and Emily Stoddard. Beth was afraid to speak, so Jess started the conversation for her,

"Beth knows she was wrong to go out in the search party, but she was so worried about little Missy. Beth has a soft heart, and it might cause her to do something stupid once in a while. She knows she was wrong, but she meant right. Please accept her apology. She will pay for your boots, Mr. Stoddard; they are stained with blood from her blisters. Please go easy on her, she's a good kid."

Dad Judd was listening with John and Emily as Jess pleaded Beth's case. Everyone was quiet when he finished. Dad Judd was smirking under his hand and he noticed John and Emily had their mouths covered too.

"Well, Beth," John Stoddard said as he let out a big sigh, "seems as though you've got an attorney who thinks we should be lenient with you, and has put you at the mercy of the court. All right, Mr. Attorney, what do you think her punishment should be?"

Whoops, Jess thought to himself, *what would Jake say?*

Jess paused and looked at the Stoddards and then back to Beth. She was looking miserable as she waited for sentencing, and his dad wasn't giving him any help, just sitting there resting his chin on his palm, with his fingers over his mouth.

"Well, she did a lot of back breaking 'working the woods'; she really did work hard, and I think a good bath and sent to bed early would be adequate correction in view of her time served." Jess announced.

The two Johns and Emily could no longer contain themselves, and started laughing out loud.

"You are going to make a fine attorney, Jess," Mr. Stoddard told him, "I lower the gavel, it is so ordered."

On the way back to the mountain, John told his son how proud of him he is and what a good job he had done in Beth's defense.

"John's right, Jess," his dad told him, "You are going to make a fine lawyer."

Jess welled up so much that dad could feel his son's satisfaction with his 'first case' without even looking at him.

As Beth lay on her bed, all cleaned up and comfortable, she could hardly believe how Jess had come to her defense. He's not such a bad fellow after all.

But, her thoughts went back to another male, and her terror of men swelled up in her mind again, and she wept softly as she buried her face in her pillow.

A City Hospital Trip

The ATV rolled up to Ira's home about 8 o'clock. He came out and jumped in the vehicle and the two men headed for their doctor's appointments. Ira was looking a bit concerned – almost like an animal that wasn't sure where its master was taking it.

Josie had done a decent job cleaning Ira's wounds, but Doc Lowery cleaned them more, then he started the injections. Ira squirmed as the doctor put the Rabies Immune Globulin right into his arm at the big injury site. But, the shoulder shots weren't so bad. Doc scheduled Ira's next four appointments, and then turned to Jake.

As he perused Jake's wounds he shook his head, "Jake, these wounds are to the bone in spots and the x-ray shows foreign matter. I'm going to put compression bandages on them, and you are to go immediately to City Hospital. Plus your loss of blood will require an IV or two to get your body going again. I'll call ahead to the hospital and tell them you'll be there in a couple of hours. Do either of you want something for pain?"

Jake shook his head no, but Ira took some as a 'just in case'.

"Pain medication makes a person goofy, and I've got a trip to take." Jake answered.

"Do you want me to drive you to City Hospital?" Ira asked Jake, who shook his head no as he headed toward Ira's home to drop him off.

Then Jake headed toward the little mobile home in the woods.

Angela came running out and grabbed her man. Her arms felt good to him as he held her tight. She tried to look at his arm, but doc had wrapped it so much that she couldn't see anything.

After a few minutes of just holding each other, Jake began to speak, "Can you get Kelli to watch your mom today if Carrie has to leave? I have to go to City Hospital to get some stitches."

"I'm sure Kelli will. Carrie is suppos' ta be home most of the day, but I'll tak to Kelli an' let 'er know whas goin' on." Angela answered.

"I'll be taking the bike, so meet me at the road in about a half-an-hour, OK?" He asked his Lady.

"I sure will." She agreed. Angela had never been on a motorcycle, and she was excited, even though she was worried about him driving with his bandaged arm. However, she knew her Jake could handle any situation.

Jake filled in his mom and dad as Josie was helping him put his helmet on. Dad secured one to the side of the bike for Angela. Jake put a blanket in one of his saddlebags. Mam grabbed some energy bars and stuffed them in one of his bags, along with two bottles of water. Mam noticed his weaving in pain, so she and John placed their hands on his shoulders and prayed for traveling mercies and help with his pain. Then she gave him a big long hug, and dad squeezed his neck as they told him how much they love him. Their actions made Jake feel comfortable as he headed toward the elevator.

"Josie dear," John remarked to his wife, "I think it's time for Angela to have the pass code, she definitely has a Judd heart."

Josie smiled and nodded affirmatively, "I think it is about time I meet my new daughter."

Angela heard the beautiful piano music as she approached Kelli Armstrong's mobile home about fifty feet from hers. She and Kelli have been best friends since birth and Kelli will be her Maiden of Honor when she and Jake get married. Their parents had even been best friends since before they were born, and the two families have always looked after each other like kin.

Kelli plays both the accordion and the piano as she sings with them. Angela plays the guitar and the violin. When the families' get together they have jamborees, like the one for Angela's twenty-first birthday, the day Jake first saw those turquoise eyes that mesmerized him. Kelli has a younger brother and sister. Kelli's younger sister, Pam, is almost a twin to her, about five feet four inches and a hundred and ten pounds. They both have the curly auburn hair and hazel eyes that change color with their moods.

Kelli's sibling ages are reversed, however, from Angela's siblings. Kelli's brother – Will – is seventeen, and her sister – Pam - is eighteen. The two girls are only two months apart, and Kelli likes to tease Angela about being older than she is. Pam and Mike both graduate this spring along with Billy Carson. Mike has decided he is going to go into the Air Force; he wants to be able to send money home to care for his mother. Pam hasn't yet decided what she wants to do but her passion is writing.

Billy Carson adores animals, and in the back of his mind he would like to be a veterinarian. He's planning on saving all the money from his summer job. Coming up 'the hard way' he knows you have to work for anything you get, and he's not afraid of work. He can often be seen just cleaning areas of the forest of debris just for fun.

Will and Carrie will graduate next spring. Will plays the fiddle and the harmonica, like Jake and Todd, along with drums. Pam plays the piano too. Carrie loves the violin, but Mike has never really gotten heavily into an instrument; he does play a trumpet and a harmonica, usually in secret, and has a good voice. Most generally when you approach the two homes in the woods you will hear music from everywhere. It's a way of life.

While sitting with Orpha, Kelli often plays the accordion to her. Orpha keeps time to the music with her right arm bouncing, and a smile as good as her distorted face can produce. Orpha was very musical before the stroke that paralyzed her; she taught many of the Woods People to play instruments. She has had a colostomy bag since the stroke. Doc Lowery comes out to the cabin once a month to check on Orpha and be sure everything is going smoothly. Doc trained all six kids in the care of Orpha, and so far they've done a good job.

Kelli's dad, Walter, is a traveling salesman and gone a lot of the time. He sells Photovoltic Cells. That's how many of the Woods People get their power.

Her mother, Nelli, is very backward and rarely talks to anyone. Usually when someone comes to the house she disappears to her bedroom. She is not very educated, and has become more of a hermit since her best friend, Orpha, became disabled. She can often be seen sitting quietly with her friend, sometimes for hours. She will even read to Orpha, kid's books she has memorized because she doesn't know the words in big books. When she comes to a word she doesn't know, she will make one up.

Angela quickly filled Kelli in on what was happening and Kelli said of course she would be glad to keep an eye on Orpha and the 'kids'.

The beautiful green Gold Wing glistened in the sun as it pulled up to the corner where Angela was already waiting. Jake's heart went up into his throat again as he caught her eyes.

Jake had special ordered his Gold Wing. They usually only come in five colors, Candy Black Cherry, Metallic Deep Blue, Silver, Pearl Yellow and Titanium, but he wanted Emerald Green Metallic. His green machine has all the perks including Linked Navigation System, an XM Radio, an airbag system and an intercom between the helmets. There are beautiful chrome sidebars and a good-sized windshield to deflect the bugs from the teeth and eyes.

Jake handed Angela the helmet and helped her put it on. Her glistening red hair streamed from the bottom of the helmet's edge like a waterfall.

This is going to be my wife, he was thinking to himself, Lord how did I deserve her?

She wasn't sure how to get on, but it didn't take her too long to get the idea that she just throws her leg over the seat, grabs Jakes shoulders and pulls herself up into the cradle. He showed her the exhaust manifold and told her to be sure and keep her leg away from it - that it gets really hot. He told her that the roll bars on the side were all right to put her feet on if she needed to move. But, the little pedals he flipped out on each side were the actual foot rests. They were off.

Somehow Jake didn't dwell on the often-excruciating pain coming from his arm, especially the spot with the sticker, Angela's touch was a wonderful anesthetic; she kept kissing his neck, and it made him purr. The pain mostly sucker punched him when he veered right in his turns because it pulled the left arm forward. Even with all the padding Doc Lowery had put on his arm, the blood was seeping through by the time he pulled into the parking lot of City Hospital.

He chained the bike to one of the big pillars holding lights far above the parking lot, and then locked both of their helmets on to the sides.

Angela surprised him by saying, "Lord, pleaz protect Jake's bike whilst we are in th' hospital."

Yep, this is his lady.

Apparently the Emergency Room personnel recognized Jake as he stepped in to the lobby, and pushed a gurney up to him and patted it.

"Do you want to wait out here?" A nurse asked Angela.

"No, I'll go in with my man." She said authoritatively.

Jake smirked and winked at her.

Without any fanfare he was rolled to the x-ray department, while an Admissions Clerk was getting his information on the run. Jake really felt strange, lying on a bed and being pushed down the hallways - by girls. Angela had a grip on the side of the gurney, and no one would beat her off of it.

A Registered Nurse started an IV in his arm, but with the other arm in so much pain he didn't even notice the stick. The bag hanging on the rack that had wheels was following right along beside him, with a bar attaching it to the side of the gurney. Another lady, apparently from the lab, was taking blood in vials for testing from his good arm.

Reluctantly Angela had to wait in the hallway as Jake got several x-rays of his left arm, then he was pushed back out into the hallway with Angela to wait for the radiologist to give the verdict.

A doctor with green pajamas and a green hat to match went into the x-ray department. After several minutes he came back out and up to Jake.

"Hello, Mr. Judd," I'm Doctor Griffin, "you have a small fracture in your ulna. That is the smaller of the two bones between your wrist and elbow. You have two bones in your forearm, one's on the outside and the second ones on the inside and the weight of the big cat fractured the one on the outside. There is a slight displacement and a foreign object, so I'll have to cast it as soon as I clean it up and remove the foreign object. Do you have any questions?"

Jake took offense at how Doc Griffin seemed to be talking down to him – explaining what the ulna bone is.

Trying to be catty-nice, Jake replied, "No, I was pretty sure I had an ulna fracture; concluded by the reference of the sticker in my arm, and with a displacement because my little finger phalanges are showing a slight anomaly at the distal end upon movement. And please, Doctor, call me Jake, my dad is Mr. Judd."

The doctor smirked, and then smiled at Jake as he told the nurses to take Jake to the operating room.

"Have you eaten today, Jake?" The doctor asked.

"Yea, about six this morning." The reposed man answered.

"Well, we'll have to give you something for nausea so you won't wake up sick and vomiting." The doctor informed him.

Dr. Griffin walked beside Jake as he questioned him for more information as to what had happened. It was obvious that the doctor was curious.

"That's an amazing story, Jake," the doctor said, "I'm going to have to admit you for the night, you need to be watched. I'll do the Rabies Immune Globulin while you are asleep, the foreign object looks suspiciously like a cat fang stuck in your bone, I think that's your sticker, and what caused the fracture. You'll have to follow up with Dr. Lowery for your completion of treatment. You are dehydrated and your blood count is way down from your blood loss. I want you to have several IV's over night and I'll order some pain medication put in them."

"Thanks, Dr. Griffin," Jake responded, "but I don't want any pain medication, just fix the arm."

The doctor looked smilingly at him for a few seconds, and then told the nurses to do as Jake requested.

"What about the young lady with you, may I discuss your treatment with her?" Dr. Griffin asked.

"Absolutely," Jake responded, "Angela is my soon to be wife, and she can know everything about me – and please save the cat's tooth for her."

The Admissions Clerk was back again with more forms for Jake to sign, including an Admission Agreement, a Surgery Agreement and insurance information.

In the waiting room the big man got stripped and put into a gown that barely covered his buttocks, and was opened in the back. Jake wasn't happy with this gown made for short people, and the rear air conditioning. He grabbed the blanket off the gurney and wrapped it around himself before anyone could peek at anything not his or her business.

After he was dressed for surgery, they let Angela back into the Surgery Waiting Room and Jake and his love were finally alone for a few moments.

"Call Mam, please, Angela, and ask her to call Ira and fill him in." Jake said to his lady as she was holding his good hand real tight.

"I will, ri'ht away," she responded, "an' Mam can ask Ira ta go an' tell Kelli wha's happenin'."

"Good," Jake uttered to her as his eyelids were getting heavy from the anesthesia in his IV, "I love you My Lady, and I'll see you as soon as I wake up. You need to go get something to eat. Get the wallet out of my pants and hang onto it, there is money in it if you need something."

"I luv y'u too, my soon ta be husban' Jake an' I'll be ri'ht here when ya wakes up." She assured him as she kissed his forehead, his cheek, nose and then his lips. He didn't need anymore anesthetic, he was already in heaven.

A Long Distance Meeting

As Mam opened her ringing cell, a soft voice said, "Hello, Mam? This's Angela Crabtree, an' they're gonna hav' ta do surgery on Jake. His arm bone is cracked an' he has a cat's tooth in it."

Josie took a deep breath as she chose her words carefully knowing Angela was emotional and frightened, "Hi Honey, thank you for calling me, Jake will be all right, how are you?"

"I'm OK." Angela responded.

"I'm so glad to finally meet you, Angela, even long distance. It's not the best of circumstances, but Jake's tough, and he will be all right," Josie said with comforting words, "so they will be keeping him overnight I assume."

"Yas Mam, they need ta watch him caus' he los' so much of 'is blood, they're givin' him IV's, an' I'm stayin' with 'im in his room so 'ell be ok." Angela told Josie, "Will ya pleaz call Ira an' 'ave 'im go tell Kelli wha's goin' on? An' we'll be home tomorrow."

"I sure will Angela, and we'll keep you both in prayer. Please come home to see me when you two get back to town, I want to meet you in person, and give you a hug." Josie told Angela.

Angela's worries over meeting Mam were gone, she felt welcome, and right. She would finally be going to Jake's home.

Josie called Ira, but Ira was sleeping.

"His pain had gotten so bad that he had to take some of the medication from Dr. Lowery, and he's really sound asleep," Todd said to her, "but what do you need done? I can do it."

Josie thanked Todd for his consideration, and told him what

was going on and that she would like for him to go and fill in Kelli and the 'kids.' That visit was sure a welcome request for Todd.

"Certainly will Mrs Judd." Todd said as they hung up. He grabbed the keys to his old beat up Toyota, it's supposed to be grey, but with all the cancer on it it's hard to tell, and headed for the Woods. His old car has considerable miles on it, but still keeps running, and seems to be good on the ruts off the road in the woods. It also gets very good gas mileage, which is wonderful because he and Ira only work part-time at the Mark's Mill, so neither one earns very much money. Todd still has a dream of becoming a Draftsman and designing things. Isaiah Marks has told Todd before that if the Mill's business ever really 'picks up' he might consider helping him with his schooling. But things are slow around Raincroft.

The melodious sounds of the accordion were escaping through the door and windows of the small mobile home as Todd pulled into the makeshift driveway. In the front door, he could see Kelli sitting on a small sofa with her instrument. He pulled the harmonica out of his shirt pocket and started blowing into it as he stepped through the open door. Kelli smiled at him and kept playing as he joined her. Pam came out from her bedroom and started singing as they played. Pretty soon both Kelli and Todd were singing too. Now they had a trio. Of course Todd couldn't play and sing at the same time, but Kelli's music never wavered. Her long fingers were moving over the black and white keys on the right side of her instrument with precision as her other hand pushed buttons on the left as she worked the bellows.

Todd has a beautiful deep baritone voice, and his music timing is perfect. Pam sang more of an alto, and Kelli was a low soprano. Their voices blended wonderfully.

Before long they were gathering more of an audience than could fit into the small room, so they moved to the porch. A few neighbors had gathered outside, and all were singing now. One thing about the Woods People, they love their music, and even though most have never had a music lesson in their lives, they all seemed to be able to harmonize in tune.

It was when Carrie and Mike joined them that Todd realized he had forgotten his mission; both kids were there now, but what about

Orpha? Todd headed over to check on Orpha and soon Kelli was running to catch up with him.

"What's going on?" She asked Todd, "Any word on Jake yet?"

"Yes, Jake will be staying in the hospital overnight; his arm is pretty serious and going to need surgery. It even has a cat fang in it." He responded.

He finished telling her as much as he knew as they were walking up on Orpha's porch. She was sitting in the familiar wheel chair and her right hand was still keeping time to the music she had been listening to.

"Hi Orpha, how's it going today?" Todd asked her as he sat down on a chair beside her, "You're really enjoying the music, huh? I remember when you used to play the piano. You played so well. One of these days you will be playing again, you just keep that in mind."

Kelli was touched at how Todd was always so nice to Orpha. "You don't act as mean as you look." She paused a few moments before she continued," are you still drawing designs on everything within reach?"

"Well, sometimes, - I still haven't given up the dream of being an architect. But that takes money and as you know money is hard to come by right now." He responded in a slightly sad tone.

As they walked back over to Kelli's home, she assured him she would keep an eye on things until Angela got back. The four 'kids' were sitting on the front porch. Will Armstrong was watching Todd, somewhat afraid - but mostly curiously. Mike and Carrie Crabtree had gotten used to seeing a mountain man around with Jake's visits. Pam Armstrong really just couldn't be bothered; she likes to be in her own little world and is always too busy journalizing everything she witnesses to be sociable.

"There's going to be an Exchange on the 21st of next month, how about us doing a jamboree in the amphitheater? Should draw a crowd." Todd was inquiring joyfully. His idea was well received; everyone thought it sounded like fun.

"I'll ask Mr. Bloom if he can roll his piano out and join us," Kelli agreed, "or at least let someone roll it out for him."

Todd thanked Kelli for her help, then left.

It seemed like forever that Angela sat alone waiting for word. Every once in a while a nurse would check with her to see if she wanted anything. She always answered no; she would wait and eat with Jake. Each time she saw a nurse come out of the surgery door, she thought there was news of Jake, but they always walked on past her. It was so hard to sit there and know they were cutting on her man, and he was asleep and didn't know what was going on.

Angela was trying to read the magazines laying in the waiting room, but about all she could do was look at the pictures.

Jake said Mam will teach me ta read an' write – an' cook. She thought to herself totally thrilled with the idea. She had already met Dad Judd, and he was really neat, and she knew Mam would be also. Her mother had been incapacitated since she was young. She had really never had the instruction of a mother and was looking forward to a good relationship with Josie. The only cooking she knew was opening a can of soup, or making hot dogs, or make stew in the crock pot.

Angela's eyelids kept trying to get heavy on her, but she would rearrange herself to wake up. About three hours later, the surgery door opened.

Dr. Griffin walked up to her and said, "Jake is doing good, Angela, there was a lot of repair work to do in the tendons. He will be in recovery for about two hours, and then he will go to a private room. The nurses will show you where they will be taking him. Here's something Jake wanted you to have – the cat's tooth. I pried it out of the bone it had gotten stuck in when the cat attacked Jake, which is what actually caused the fracture in his arm. With the many hundreds of pounds pressure in the big cat's jaws, it is amazing that the bone was not reduced to pieces, or he could have lost his arm completely. The tooth's cleaned up. Jake's going to have a pretty good sized bandage on his arm, and won't be able to bend it for a while, but he's going to be all right. I'm ordering a PRN pain prescription for him, just in case the pain gets too bad. PRN means only if he wants it."

Angela thanked the doctor for his report and for taking good care of Jake. However, not being able to bend his arm was a bit disconcerting to her. But her man could take care of any situation, he knows everything.

Josie answered immediately when Angela called in the report to her.

"Hi honey," she said as she answered, "how is Jake and how are you?"

"Jake's doin' good. Th' doctor jus' giv me th' big cat's tooth. It's ugly." Angela filled Mam in on the rest of what the doctor had said.

"Good thing Ira thought fast, huh?" Mam said to her.

"Yea, he couda lost an arm, or worser." Angela replied.

"How are you, Angela," Mam continued, "have you eaten anything yet?"

"No, Mam, I'll eat with Jake when he wakes up. I hope he cain drive home OK." She answered.

"Well, Honey, just call if you need Dad to come and get you guys, he can hook up the bike trailer and be there in a couple of hours," Josie told her, "so you quit your worrying, everything is going to be all right."

"Yes, Mam." Angela agreed.

Angela jumped to her feet as she saw them bringing Jake's gurney out of the Recovery Room door. He was trying to open his eyes as he felt her presence. She took his good hand and kissed it. He smiled and drifted back to sleep. His soul was comforted by her presence.

Another hour had passed before Jake opened his eyes again to see his lovely lady sitting there watching him.

"Hi Baby," he said to her softly, "have you eaten anything?"

"No, I'm waitin' for yu ta eat," she answered him, "but I was glad ta see an insid' torlet. Now, yu jus pleaz be quiet so ya get better faster."

He drifted back to sleep as Angela prepared for a long night. A nurse brought her a blanket – it was warm, and a pillow. The nurse told her she had put the blanket in a thing called an autoclave to heat it and she showed Angela how to put the footrest up on the chair so she could relax.

The beautiful little red head's eyes were soon so heavy she could not control them, and she drifted off to sleep. Stress even takes a toll on the young, and her little body needed refreshing. She was sure glad Jake had showed her how to use the cell phone so she could keep in contact with Mam. She instinctively knew Mam was like Jake and could make anything ok.

Several times during the night a nurse would come in, check Jake and give him another antibiotic. When the little bag hanging on the pole with wheels got empty a shrill whistle would sound. The first one scared Angela, but the nurse explained to her that it was just to let the nurses know it was time to change his IV.

Jake was sitting on the edge of his bed when Angela opened her eyes.

"What ar' ya doin' up?" She asked him.

"Waiting to get unhooked so we can get out of here," he told her, "I'm doing fine, but I can't go to the toilet. This catheter is going for me, and I don't like it. I want to go see Missy, Keith and Laura before we leave."

Angela was surprised when the nurse brought her a breakfast tray too. She hadn't eaten since early the previous morning, and she was starved.

"Always herd hospital food's not good – but it's delicious." She told Jake, who was also eating everything on his plate.

Jake asked the nurse to remove the needles from his arm and told her he'll pull the catheter out, so he could move around a bit.

"You can't remove the catheter, it has a bulb on the inside that has to be deflated and Dr. Griffin would like to get one more IV into you. He is sending you home on two antibiotics to prohibit infection." The nurse informed him as she worked.

Then without warning she deflated and took the catheter out. Jake was surprised and irritated, but glad it was done.

With all the hardware off of him, Jake stood up. He was a bit woozy as Angela grabbed his good arm.

"Like you could hold me up," he chuckled at her, but she acted like she was superwoman as she stabilized him, "you're a determined little gal."

The nurses waited about an hour and a half before they would let him go; they said they were still waiting for the antibiotics to come up from the pharmacy. Jake figured they were stalling to keep an eye on him and feed in the additional IV. By the time the medicine arrived he was walking pretty steady and asked what room the Grants were in.

"205 A&B," the nurse told him, "apparently dad and daughter are in the same room."

Jake put on the rest of his clothes and boots, and he an Angela started for room 205, in spite of the nurse's words that she would go for a wheelchair. Angela called Josie again and told her they were going to see the Grants and then start home.

My, Josie thought, *what a real sweetie. My son is really being blessed with this young lady. I'm so anxious to meet her this afternoon. I'll have some special honey biscuits baked for them.*

As they approached room 205 they could hear the little girl trying to talk.

They heard her say "Doggie" and "Muffy."

Missy repeated the words several times as they walked up to the room. Obviously she was talking about two different things that had made a strong impression on her. Her bed was raised up to where she was sitting almost upright in it; her little leg was in a cast from her hip to her foot. Laura was sitting on the side of the bed when they walked in. When Missy saw Jake, she didn't cower this time, she smiled at him.

"Jake," Laura said to Missy, "Jake."

"Yake," The little angel repeated, "Yake, Doggie, Muffy."

It seemed like she was trying to tell Jake she remembers the two animals. Missy seemed to also recognize Angela as the lady who helped pull her up to safety, and smiled at her.

"That's Angela." Laura said to her, but the little girl didn't try that word.

The big mountain man's heart melted as he heard the little girl say his name, and try to tell him what had happened to her. Jake didn't get too close to Missy, he didn't want to scare her or bring bad memories back. Everything he and Ira had been through was totally worth the trouble when he saw she was all right - and said his name. He could hardly wait to tell Ira she is talking.

Jake walked up to Keith's bed and could see he had a cast on the same leg as Missy, also from his waist to his foot. Both men grabbed each other's hands in a welcoming grip.

"Our daughter is fine, and our family is in tact because of you, Jake. I don't know how I can ever thank you." Keith's words were becoming hard to say as the tears started ruining his vision.

"It's ok, man, my pleasure." The big man replied. Angela held up the cat's tooth for Keith and Laura to see. Missy wanted to see it too, so Angela let her hold it.

"Cat, cat, Yake," Missy said. Apparently Missy had seen the big cat. Was it when the cat was dead on the ground – or – when it had attack Jake – or – had it tried to get in to the cave and the lady wolf had fended it off? Usually a wolf is no match for a mountain lion, but in her small cave, the lady wolf had an advantage. The footing for the big lion was almost non-existent.

"You look like you've been through a grinder, what's the verdict?" Keith asked.

Jake told them about the surgery, and how he had to wear his cast for about a month, "It's gonna interfere with what I have to do, but I guess this too shall pass. I've got to get in shape to go back into the canyon. I've got a job to finish and two slimemolds to catch."

Keith and Laura both knew what he meant. Keith told him to be sure and let him know what he could do to help.

They stayed and talked to the Grants for about forty-five minutes, then left to go home. As they were leaving the room Missy called after them, "Bye Yake." 'Yake' turned his head to look back at her as he whispered, "Bye, Bye, Little Missy."

Angela saw the tears in his eyes, and her heart almost exploded. The bike was still there all right, helmets and all. Angela had to help him put on his helmet, and he wasn't much good helping her with his one hand.

"You're a good helpmeet My Lady." He told her as she finished tightening his chin strap.

She climbed on the back and nuzzled up to her man as he started the emerald bike. It felt so good to lean against him and to know he is going to be all right. With his arm in a cast and slightly bent, Jake had to lean way forward for his hand to reach the left handlebar and clutch.

Jewelry Shopping &
A Meeting

Instead of heading out of town as Angela expected, they pulled into a shopping mall, straight up to a jewelry store. Jake put the kickstand down, stepped off the bike and took Angela's hand to help her crawl off the bike. She helped him take his helmet off and then took hers off. He had shown her at the hospital how to hold them close to the bike to lock them in place securely. Then the two held hands as they walked into the jewelry store.

Both hearts were pounding as they started looking at wedding ring sets. Angela was amazed at the prices. Jake had been checking around Raincroft for rings, but nothing caught his eye, besides he really didn't want the whole town to know how much he was paying for his wife's rings.

Evidently the jeweler didn't think they were serious customers by their looks, and really didn't pay much attention to them, other than watch them out of the corner of his eye. This was ok though; they could look at every set without being bothered – and they did. Then like clockwork they both spied the perfect set.

"We'll take that set," Jake announced, "let's try them on the lady."

The jeweler unlocked the case and nervously took the set of rings out of the display case. Jake almost had to pry them out of the salesman's fingers to put them on Angela's third finger of her left hand. They both looked at them for a few moments as they kept exchanging smiley glances at each other. Jake was enjoying, in a slightly sic way, the nervous man's eyes remaining glued onto the set of rings, as if to be sure they both came back to him.

"Perfect," Angela whispered.

"Perfect," Jake agreed, "how much are they?"

"Fourteen hundred plus tax and fitting," The salesman answered.

"They fit perfectly." Angela informed the salesman.

The rings were two-tone 14K gold. The engagement ring had a large round solitaire in the center of the engagement ring, with a smaller stone on each side, and a baguette diamond on each outer side. The wedding band had a curve in the top of the band so it would fit snugly against the engagement ring. It had four diamonds to match the ones on each side of the big diamond, and baguettes on each side like the engagement ring. They were really beautiful, and he could tell his lady was committing every detail to memory. The tag on the engagement ring said 0.810 center stone, so it was almost one full karat.

"Now," the big man continued, "we want a two-tone man's ring also, no diamonds, I do rough work and want one without stones."

"We have some nice ones over in that case," he said pointing across the aisle, and clutching the wedding rings tight in his fist as if they might come up missing, "do you know your ring size?"

"Big." Jake smirked as the man set the ring case on the back counter – out of reach.

"Let's measure your ring finger," the salesman continued as he started with a size 12-ring hoop, "we'll have to beat that."

The man tried a 13, and then a 14. The 14 fit nicely.

"I have two choices in size 14 right now, and one is a two-tone that will match your misses." The salesman said as he took out the ring and held it up to Jake. Angela pried it from the man's fingers and placed it on Jake's finger. It was a bit tight going on, but it fit after it got over the big knuckle.

"Let's see the wedding rings again," Jake asked so they could compare them together.

Both thought the match was perfect. The ring was 14K gold with a white gold rope band through the center of the ring.

"Feels funny," Jake told Angela, "never had a ring on before, -but I'm going to be happy to get used to it. We'll take it."

"Now," Jake continued, "I want a gold chain that will fit around my neck and a matching one to fit my lady."

"We have some nice herringbone chains right over here," He said as he pointed toward the end of the store, putting the rings back safely on the rear counter.

Jake and Angela looked at every one of the chains, and then picked out matching ones they both liked, although she wasn't sure why they each needed one. She tried the big one on Jake and his fit good around his big neck. Then she tried a smaller one on herself, and it fit perfectly, so Jake told the man he would take both of them.

The salesman stepped over to a cash register and started punching buttons.

"With tax your total purchase is $2,020.28. How are you going to finance the jewelry?"

"There's no financing. I don't buy anything unless I have the money to pay for it." Jake notified him as he took the wallet out of his rear pocket and told Angela to get the money out and pay for their purchases.

As she laid four five-hundred dollar bills and one fifty dollar bill on the counter, a second man came out from the back of the store with a yellow pen and started marking on the bills. Both men were still looking uneasily at the mountain man.

"Umm," The man stammered with surprise at the bills being real, "I need your name, address and telephone number."

"Well, my name's Jake Judd, my address is Box 77, Raincroft, and you don't need my phone number. I'll call you if I want to talk to you." Jake responded.

Before entering the transaction in the cash register, the man excused himself and went into the back of the store. He was gone about five minutes, then came back and entered the information in his moneybox. As the paid receipt spit out, the man seemed to have had an attitude adjustment and he started putting the jewelry in beautiful little royal blue velvet boxes. Angela's rings were in one,

Jake's ring was in another one, and the chains were each put in their own long skinny royal blue velvet boxes.

He started to put them all in one gold sack that had the name of the jewelry store on it, but Angela told him to please put Jakes ring and chain in one sack, and her rings and chain in another sack. He did so. As he handed Jake the two sacks, Jake gave Angela the one with his chain and ring, and he put the sack with her rings under his shirt and close to his heart. Angela put his ring under her blouse close to her heart. They had known what the other was thinking without a word being spoken.

As they started to leave Angela spotted a small turquoise butterfly and asked Jake if they could get it for Mam. Jake had told her how much Mam loves butterflies, just like she does. Jake bought the pin, and after the man put it in the beautiful blue velvet box and gold sack, Angela put it under her shirt by her heart too. Jake's heart was floating in the clouds as they walked out of the store to the bike. This time Angela knew how to unlock the helmets and put them on; she was really becoming his helpmeet.

"I ain't nev'r seen sa much money in my life." She said to him.

"Well, baby," he said as he looked into her eyes, "I've been saving since the first time I looked into your beautiful turquoise eyes. I knew right then that you would be my wife."

The ride back to Raincroft was very hard on Jakes broken arm. He had to lean so far forward to reach the handlebar with the front brake and clutch with his left hand that it made his arm really throb; but he was on a mission. His mother and his soon to be wife were going to meet and a butterfly pin would seal the deal. Mam would teach her new daughter-in-law to read, speak, write and cook - and home school her grandkids.

He was trying to decide whether or not he should show Angela his secret project, he would think about it as they rode, and would have a decision by the time they got to Mystery Mountain. He knew he had to keep mind over matter for pain control, and with so many thoughts going through his head, he hardly had time to dwell on the often-excruciating pains that would bounce through his arm. He could feel Angela's love radiating from her little arms tight arms around his chest.

They reached the turn-a-round and started on up the narrow path. As the thick trees cleared, the mountain showed up in the foreground. Angela was brimming with excitement. She had often thought about what was in the mountain and when she would see it. As Jake pushed the Code Buttons and the big rock tilted back Jake could feel Angela's eyes get huge. They drove quickly onto the elevator and the big rock shut them in. She looked all around her. The rock had been hollowed out, and they were now encased in it. The elevator started down as they sat silently; Angela had no words.

John and Josie were waiting for them in the garage as the elevator stopped. Oreo and Stria had joined them. The two pets could feel the excitement, and seemed to be waiting for their introduction too. Jake put the kickstands down and was grinning ear to ear as Angela helped him take his helmet off. Then take hers off and lock them both onto the bike. His arm was obviously hurting him pretty badly; Mam could see his pain in his eyes, as she gave him a great big extended hug. Then she turned her attention to Jake's little red head, and put her arms around her and gave her the same extended hug as she welcomed her new daughter home to Mystery Mountain.

"Hi Angela honey, you are so welcome, I'm so glad to finally meet you." Mam was saying.

Dad also gave Angela a hug, then introduced Oreo and Stria. Jake had told Angela about the pets, and that they were good pets and wouldn't hurt her. She knelt down and started stroking both pets as they raised their hiney's up like a cat with sheer enjoyment when her hand went down their backs. They started up the steps to the kitchen with Mam's arm around Angela's waist. The two pets were pouncing up the steps ahead of them. Jake and Dad followed. Mam and Angela were jabbering like jaybirds. Mam wanted to know everything about the soon to be mother of her grandchildren.

Mam had two Aleve ready on the table with a glass of water and a pillow. Jake picked them up, took them gratefully, and sat down at the table as he put his arm up on the pillow.

"Ya sure know how ta do thin's." Angela said to Josie.

Angela was trying to take everything in, she had no idea it was so nice in the home and that it was so spacious, plus all the marble everywhere was unbelievable. She had expected a cave, but this was no cave.

"I told the rest of the family to give us some time together before they come down," Mam grinned at Angela, "some of them can get pretty noisy, and I want to talk to you peacefully first."

Angela knew about the 'discussions' between Uncle Ernie and Joe, and how they get louder as they progress, each trying to make the other one hear them.

About fifteen minutes later Jani came into the kitchen. The two girls had met, but never been formally introduced.

"This is Jani," Josie introduced the two young ladies, "and this is Angela."

Jani walked up and gave Angela a hug, and she responded with a big hug back. One by one the rest of the family moseyed in and were introduced to Jake's lady. All were so warm and welcoming to her that Angela felt right at home.

Angela noted there were bar-be-cue ribs on the grill, with corn on the cob and baked potatoes. The table was all set like they were expecting someone important. Angela looked at the hot honey buns and knew they must be as good as Jake had said they were – his favorite. Talk was exciting as they all ate. It had been a very busy few days, and there was a lot to say, especially about the horrifying trip into the canyon. Mam, Jani and Angela got along like they have been friends all their lives.

After dinner was cleaned up and Angela had seen her first dishwasher, and learned how to properly load it, she asked if she could see the chapel. Mam and Jani both nodded yes. The three ladies headed for the elevator because Mam knew Angela was tired and there were a lot of steps to climb to the top floor. Jake stepped into the elevator too, as if he couldn't let his little red head out of his sight. Dad followed. Mam noted how precious their feelings for each other are and how they already can almost read each other's thoughts.

The three ladies sat down on the wooden benches in front. Jake and Dad sat down on the back ones.

"I can see I need to make about three more seats," his dad said to Jake, "we've got seven, but how soon will we need the eighth one?"

Jake knew his dad was fishing as he replied, "Soon, Dad, soon."

Angela took out the package over her heart and handed it to Josie, who was a bit surprised at the welcome little sack. She took the blue velvet box out of the golden sack, and opened it carefully as Angela was wiggling around with excitement like a cute little poodle. When the lid came up on the velvet box, the little butterfly seemed to be glistening at Josie; perhaps it was just the tears she was looking through.

"It's beautiful Angela," Mam choked out, "what an unexpected blessing. It's wonderful; help me pin it on please."

Angela turned and took the little butterfly and pinned it on Mam as she said, "Jake paid for it, but I did pick it out."

"It's from both of you, and it matches your turquoise eyes, and that makes it even more wonderful." Josie remarked, "It's extraordinary, thank you both so very much."

Angela glanced back at Jake a few times as they chatted; she could see him laying his head against the wall for support.

"I need ta go home now so Kelli won be so worried an' I'm afraid fo Jake ta drive more today, so coud yu pleas' drop me off close to home Jani?" Angela asked Jani softly.

"Of course." Jani replied.

The four Judd's in the Prayer Room were really touched at how she looks after Jake. *Josie has always been that way with me.* John thought to himself.

Angela kissed and hugged her man as they got to Jani's VW. He shut the car door after his lady, and the little pink car took off for the elevator. Jake hadn't felt like showing her the special project he had been working on, he would show her when he felt more like celebrating.

Jani had the top down on her little pink car.

"I ain't nev'r been in one o thez before." She told Jani as they went down the path to the turn-a-round. As the trees started covering the little mountain road, Angela was trying to look at them all.

"I love my little bug," Jani assured her, "and some day I know you will learn how to drive too."

"But I hav' ta lern ta read firs, Jani," Angela told her, "Jake sed Mam would teach me ta read an' write an' cook. I don' wanna be a bother but I sur' do wanna lern."

Jani knew she was getting a really neat sister-in-law, and one who really loves her big brother. The two jabbered like magpies as they rode. Angela told her about how she had to quit school to take care of her mom and siblings, and her father couldn't handle her mom being not well, and left, and he has an old trailer down by the crick.   Jani was listening for any sign of a date or actual engagement.

"We'll have to do lunch sometime, Angela," Jani was saying as Jake's red head got out of the car, "do you like Mexican food?"

"I luv it, an' thans fur th' ride Jani." Angela answered.

When Jani got back home, Mam was waiting for her with questions, "What do you think of Angela? Did she give you any idea of a date?"

"No," Jani answered, "but she needs to learn to speak, read and write."

"It'll be a pleasure to teach our new little family member anything she will let me." Josie responded as she hugged her daughter.

Jake was in bed; Mam had given him two more Aleve and propped his arm up on the pillow. She kissed her big son's forehead as his eyelids got so heavy they wouldn't stay open. Right now, he was just her little boy and he is a hero. She noticed the golden sack on the nightstand and smiled. Mam was sure she knew what the pretty sack contained.

A Visit to the Sheriff's Office

As Jake walked into the Sheriff's Office about 6:30 in the morning, Deputy Homer was waiting for the boys to show up for work duty as he was doing some paperwork.

"Good – Good morning – Mr. Jake," The deputy stammered as Jake sat down in a chair across the desk from him, "I'm waiting for the boys to come in, the sheriff always gives the last arrival the worst job, so they've been pretty well on time."

"That's good, Homer," Jake answered him noting the shakiness in his voice and his hand start to scribble, "I'm here to fetch one of the boys for some fence mending. And by the way Deputy thanks for all your help finding little Missy. You did a good job, and if you're interested Jani is doing fine."

Homer about had a cow, this big man was talking to him, and he must have read his mind wanting to know how Jani is.

"Gosh, ttthanks Mr. Jake, thanks a lot, and you can have any of the boys you want," the shaking deputy responded, "and if you need anything just let me know and I'll be glad to do anything you want done. Yes Sir, you're one big hero."

Jake tried to keep from laughing.

About that time the first three boys stepped into the office. When they saw Jake they quickly went to the open cell and sat down.

"That one's Max Monroe, he's sixteen, and that's Jimmy Price, he's sixteen, and that's Ronnie Baker, he's seventeen," Homer was telling Jake as two more boys walked in and sat down in the cell, "that's Wayne Close, he's only fourteen. Wayne told us he was sixteen when he was arrested, but we found out different. And that other one is Chad Wall; he's sixteen years old. The mean one isn't here yet – that would be Sonny Boatright, he's seventeen, and doesn't like people, working or orders, and has a foul mouth. Been several people send him back because of his attitude."

The sixth kid walked in just as Homer finished. He didn't go to the cell; he went and sat down in the chair Jake had just gotten up out of as he headed for the water cooler. He acted like he thought he was king of the hill. Homer asked the kid to go sit in the cell with the others, but he ignored the deputy. Jake watched Sonny's defiance out of the corner of his eye as he took a drink from a paper cup. The kid just sat there looking pompous.

Jake walked over to him, grabbed his collar and the back of his neck, and lifted him up off the chair.

"Now, I think I heard Deputy Homer give you an order," Jake told Sonny as he pulled him over to the empty cell next to the other five boys and tossed him in head first, "it's my understanding that Deputy Homer is the boss around here, including yours. By the way, I don't like your name, Sonny Boatright, sounds like a man and you're no man. I think your new name will be Sissy Canoe. Yea, that's a good name for you, Sissy Canoe. You boys got that? That's what you are to call him from now on, understand?"

All five boys in the next cell nodded affirmatively.

"Deputy, will you please lock the door on Sissy, I want her to remain in the cell today while the other gentlemen go to work." Jake asked Deputy Homer very politely.

"Absolutely, Mr. Jake." Homer responded. "If his attitude is a bit better in the morning he will go with me to the Stoddards to mend some fences that some loose cattle broke. Otherwise he can spend tomorrow in the cell also. By the way, nothing but vegetables and water for him today." Jake added.

"Right." Homer agreed.

The kid was huskier than Homer, a really tough looking kid and a real bully, but he wasn't going to push Jake around, even with a bad arm. Jake looked at the kid's shirt pocket and saw a pack of cigarettes hiding in it. He told Homer to unlock the cell and he stepped into it as he said,

"By the way Sissy, there's no smoking in the sheriff's office, give me that pack of cigarettes."

Sonny backed up in resistance as the mountain man continued, "Now, Sissy, we can either do this little job peacefully – or not."

"Ha," Sonny retaliated, "you're not so big, you've only got one arm."

"I got you in this cell without any problem, didn't I?" Jake reminded him as his steel eyes focused on Sonny's.

"Yea, but I wasn't expecting you to touch me, now I see you." Sonny replied.

"Well, well, Sissy, to deal with you all I need are two fingers," Jake warned him, "girls are easy to take down."

You could almost see the steam coming out of Sonny's ears as he stared at the big man.

"Wanna try me Sissy?" Jake asked him very politely.

The boy looked at Jake a few more moments, then reached into his pocket and handed Jake the cigarettes.

"That's better, now sit down and shut up." Jake said to him.

The kid just stood there, but that didn't matter, he had been given some come uppins. Jake handed the cigarettes to the Deputy and told him to dispose of them. Sonny started to say something in response to Jake's order, but as Jake turned and faced him and took a couple of steps toward the cell, Sissy sat down quietly. It bothered Sonny how Jake's steel blue eyes stared directly into his; it was a bit unnerving, because he was used to everyone cowering to him.

About that time Sheriff Leo walked in.

"Well, deputy, I see you have things in control around here this morning; glad you put Sonny in a cell by himself." The sheriff said to his deputy.

"Well, sheriff," Homer came back, "I didn't do it, Mr. Jake did."

"Good," replied Leo, "what can I do for you Jake? And, did you finish your business in the City? A man called me and said you were there."

"Sure did, sheriff," Jake responded knowing now the reason for the salesman's five minute absence to the back room, "everything went fine. But, this arm is going to create a small problem fixing fences. Tomorrow, if Sissy behaves today, I'll take her with me if that's alright with you."

"It's better than all right, Jake;" the sheriff said pleasingly, "everyone else's sent him back."

"I won't," Jake assured the sheriff, "however, he just may have a broken arm or leg when I return him. I'll need to borrow a pair of your cuffs. If he won't work, since he is a prisoner, I'll have to cuff him to something to keep him from escaping."

"You got them." The sheriff chuckled.

Then Jake turned to another subject, "Any news on the hair samples yet?"

"Not yet," replied Leo, "but Leslie Stoddard has been assigned to the case since she knows the area. She should be here sometime this next week or the following one, and she will probably have any current findings in the case. She is now a Forensic Investigator."

The big man nodded as he left. "Ira and I will give her back up." Jake assured Leo.

As Jake's ATV pulled into the Stoddard ranch, John and Barstow come out to meet him.

"Looks like you've been into an argument with a wild cat," John was joshing, "you're not planning on working today are you?"

"No, just checking in," Jake assured him, "I'll be here tomorrow, and I'm bringing the ringleader of the group that tried to rape Jani. He needs some bringing up; he's a smart mouthed bully. He's going to get a lesson in hard work tomorrow."

John paused a bit before he replied, "That's Sonny Boatright?"

"Yep." Jake responded.

"His parents own a chain of motels, one of them is right there on the highway just outside of town called 'The Rainrest Motel'. I understand they have about ten of the motels scattered about the state." John informed him.

"I know the one." Jake stated.

John continued, "Even before his parents bought the Rainrest Motel a year ago and left him in charge of it, he and his sister were left to fend for themselves. He's been cutting his way through life since he was about twelve years old. Wally and Irene Boatright have been so busy making money with their motels, and not training up their children, that both kids are pretty wild. Don't know what happened to Donna, I think she's about a year younger than her brother."

"Interesting," Jake remarked, "the Bible says that kids left to themselves will bring shame to themselves and their families. That's good to know John, makes sense now, a defensive and fighting attitude. We'll both see you in the morning."

Jake had another stop to make. As he was driving he kept thanking God that his parents spent so much time with him and taught him right and wrong and love for his fellow man.

As his ATV pulled up in front of Orpha's mobile home, his beautiful lady come running out and landed in his arms even before he could get out of his vehicle.

"I'm so glad ta see ya Jake, I've bin worried, an' didn 'ave a way ta call ya," Angela was confiding, "an' I jus miss ya sa much."

As he stepped out of his ATV with Angela still clinging to him, he held his little woman close. Right now they didn't need words, only each other's touch.

Angela finally broke the silence, "How's yur arm? Bin wondern' how it was hurtin' an' if yur takin' tha pills tha hospital doc gave ya."

"I'm doing ok, and I am remembering to take the antibiotics," Jake assured her, "and the pain isn't so bad today, Mam's Aleve seems to be helping lots."

Through the door Jake could see Orpha in her wheel chair. "Let's take your mom for a ride." Jake suggested.

"OK," Angela agreed, "but th' wheels don work too good on her chair."

"Well, we'll just have to put her in the ATV then for her spin. I think we can lift her OK, I'll just pull the rig up to the front porch." Jake told her.

As he stepped back from her and pulled the ATV right up to the porch, he could see Orpha watching him.

"Now, we'll roll her chair out on the porch, and only have about four feet to lift her and we can manage that." He assured Angela.

They walked inside and Jake told Orpha he and Angela were going to take her for some fresh air. She smiled her best with her eyes, she understood.   He rolled her chair out on the porch.

"Angela will go get you a sweater so you don't get chilled." Jake told Orpha. When Angela left the room Jake added, "I'm going to pick you up now, Orpha, and put you in my ATV."

Orpha's eyes were still smiling at the big man as he picked her up out of the chair, carried her over to the ATV and sat her in the rider's seat very gently. By that time Angela was back with her sweater and Jake helped Angela put the sweater on her mother, adjust her ever-present bag and fasten the seat belt around her.

"Jake Judd," Angela said to him, "yu didn' wait fur me ta help ya. Did it hurt yur arm?"

"No baby, I'm all right, your mother doesn't weigh much at all," Jake assured his love as he kissed her on the end of her nose, "but you will have to ride 'back saddle' - in the rumble seat. There's the blanket that will help you be more comfortable."

Angela crawled up into the rumble seat, she could hold her man's neck very easily from this spot. She remembered that this is how she had clung on to his neck on the way back from the canyon rescue… - It was for sure Ira couldn't have fit in the rumble seat.

Orpha hadn't been out of her home for a very long time, and you could see her radiant countenance as the wind blew through her thinning hair and across her frail face. Her eyes sparkled like tiny lights as she looked around.

"Now Orpha," Jake was saying to her as they passed the white church, "this is where Angela and I will be getting married, and you will be sitting in the front row just like every mother of the bride does with your new dress, shoes and mother's corsage."

Angela was busting with pride, to think that someone cared enough for her to also care for her invalid mother with such gentleness.

After Jake took Angela and Orpha home he paid a visit to the Verizon wireless office on the square. Tom Crane was at his usual desk when the big man walked in.

"Hello Jake," Tom said to him, "what can I help a hero with today?"

"I need cell phone service for my soon to be wife." Jake told him.

"You mean Angela?" Tom inquired.

"Sure do Tom," Jake responded, "and I'll take that bright pink phone, with the same program I have."

"Very good, Jake, that's our best service and…."

Jake interrupted Tom; "I don't need a sales pitch. Just give me the phone, tell me the number for it and how much it's going to be."

Jake paid for the phone and the first months 'half-price' special.

"Thanks, Jake." Tom said to him as he gave him his receipt.

Jake nodded. This should keep his little lady from worrying so much, now she could call him and know he is ok. Besides she could keep in touch with Mam. He headed for home intending on charging the cell before he gave it to his lady the next day.

Work 'Force'

As Jake walked in the Sheriff's Office, he noted Sonny was not in yet. He sat down and was talking with Leo about what John Stoddard had said. The sheriff agreed that Sonny had had a rough life and no one to care about what happened to him. He also confirmed to Jake that Wayne Close is only fourteen years old and the sheriff thinks he just wanted to be part of something.

Apparently his father, Wayne Sr., had died about six months ago at the age of twenty-nine of Sickle Cell Anemia. Leo didn't know anything else except that they had bought an old trailer out in the Woods and the mother, Annabelle Close, gets a small welfare check each month. Leo told him that he understands there is a younger brother named Wilson.

"Annabelle's only about twenty-nine years old, and has a rough row to hoe." Leo added.

8:04 A.M. Sonny finally walked in and was surprised to see Jake there waiting. He assumed when he didn't show up on time Jake would pick another one of the boys to work with him. Jake noted another package of cigarettes in his pocket, and he held his hand out to Sonny to give them to him. Sonny hesitated, but with Jakes gripping eyes, he finally handed them to Jake.

"Destroy these," Jake told Sheriff Leo, "gonna be no smoking on my watch."

The sheriff took the cigarettes and mashed them in the wastebasket behind his desk.

"Now for the cuffs." Jake added. Leo handed him a set.

"Let's go." Jake said sternly to Sonny.

After taking his time to pause and draw a couple of deep sighs, Sonny slowly headed to the ATV Jake was already waiting in.

As Sonny got in the ATV Jake was saying, "Fasten your seatbelt."

"Don't do seatbelts." Sonny responded.

Again Jake's steel eyes stared at him, as Jake grabbed the kid's knee and squeezed.

"Stop it, you can't do that to me, ouch, let go." Sonny was reaching for the seat belt as Jake added, "You can either make a good day or a really bad one, and it's up to you."

"Wait 'til my folks hear how you're treating me – they'll sue you." He was warning the big man.

Jake didn't even acknowledge the kid's objections.

John Stoddard came out to the ATV as it pulled in. He was telling Jake that something spooked the cattle over night, Barstow thought he had heard a coyote, and there was quite a bit of fencing needing repair. Some of the cattle had gotten out, but he and Barstow had rounded up most of them. A couple couldn't be found, but Barstow was going to keep looking.

"Great," remarked Sonny, "now I suppose I get to herd cattle."

Both Jake and John ignored his comment.

Jake introduced 'Sissy' to John and told him the kid was there under protest, and any monkey business he would be cuffing him to something. Jake also warned that the kid had a big mouth, so ignore screams. However, if Sissy started with his foul language, Jake would just have to take action to clean it up. The dirty looks coming from Sonny would be a bit comical if Jake weren't so serious.

"Let's go." Jake told the kid as he jumped out of the ATV.

Slowly Sonny got out too.

Jake took out a post hole digger, the kind with two steel jaws at the bottom that act like scissors as you hit the ground with them. Then you open the two handles and the dirt trapped between the jaws falls out. John Stoddard usually uses a hydraulic posthole digger that hooks up to his tractor. He didn't say a word; however, he knew the big man had his own thoughts.

"There's a pair of gloves in the rumble seat if you want them." Jake told Sonny.

"H….no," the kid responded. "I ain't using a 'blankity blank' thing of yours."

"Suit yourself. - John, please turn around." Jake answered in a monotone voice.

Jake bent over and picked up something. Then smacked the pile of dung from the roaming cattle across the kid's mouth. Sonny was shocked, and started spitting and sputtering and screaming.

"Now," Jake told him, "if you are going to be a potty mouth, you'll get real potty mouth treatment."

John Stoddard still had his back toward the two.

"Wait'll my folks hear about this, they'll sue you." He warned Jake again.

"Do what? It's just your word against mine, and you are a known liar." Jake responded.

"He saw it." The kid was pointing to John, who replied, "I'm afraid I didn't see anything young man."

Jake and Sonny went on out to the corral as Sonny kept choking and gagging. Jake started showing him how to dig and sink poles.

"Usually we use a level to see how straight upright they are, but since these are just log fences we don't have to." Jake was telling him.

The kid started sweating, so Jake told him he could stop for a drink of water. After about fifteen minutes Jake ordered him back to work. They worked for about another hour when he felt the kid was up to something.

Suddenly the kid bolted toward the woods. Within a few seconds the mountain man was in front of him and grabbed him from behind the trunk of a tree.

"Well, since you like it so well in the woods, I guess you'll just have to stay here for a spell while I work." Jake informed him as he slapped the cuffs on one of Sonny's wrists, stretched his other arm around the tree and locked the cuff onto his other wrist.

"Now you can just 'hug a tree' until I get ready to leave." Jake told the young captive.

"You can't do this to me, you're holding me captive. There are wild animals here in the woods, they'll eat me." The kid was hollering at Jake.

"They might." Jake answered as he calmly walked back out of the woods.

Barstow was talking with John as Jake got back into the corral, and Jake hollered over at them, "The kid's hugging a tree."

They both laughed. Jake couldn't work too much; the movement of his shoulder made the pain really bad, so he, John and Barstow just stood around talking. In the background they could hear screams coming from the woods – that they were ignoring, he was just getting a lot of frustration out of him.

"Jake," John was saying, "I want to get a hold of Todd Carson. Do you know if he is still doing drafting? Beth thinks we should put together a petting zoo she can manage, and I'd like for Todd to see what he thinks about a small barn and a nice pen for them."

"I don't have Todd's phone number, but let me write down Ira's," Jake responded, "and how is Beth doing now?"

"Great." Barstow chimed in.

"So this petting zoo is her idea?" Jake questioned. "Pretty good one I think. Jess said she had a pretty scary trip to the woods, but he thinks she is coming along nicely."

"It is Beth's idea," John answered, "she's doing alright. In fact, she's progressing faster in her recovery than we thought she would. Like most kids, she just needed someone to care what happened to her. Yep, you can tell Jess she's doing well on her probation."

All three men laughed.

After Jake had lingered what he felt was long enough, he went back to fetch Sonny who had calmed down. The kid was obviously exhausted and had slumped down the tree and was leaning into it face first.

As he uncuffed the kid Jake told him, "Let's go get something to eat, do you like McDonald's? Then I'll take you back to the Sheriff and tell him you are done for the day."

When they got into the ATV, the big man didn't even have to

tell Sonny to buckle His seat belt, he did it first.

"Half a day isn't too bad for your first day." Jake was saying, but Sonny didn't say anything back to Jake, who noted that Sonny kept rubbing his wrists and his one thumb.

At McDonald's they just went through the drive-through and ate in the ATV. The two really didn't look like they should be in a clean restaurant.

When they walked into the Sheriff's Office, Sonny walked straight to the cell and lay down.

"Guess he's tired, huh?" Sheriff Leo remarked.

"Yep, not used to man's work," Jake answered as he noticed the kid was still rubbing a spot on the inside of his thumb, "looks like he may have a blister, do you have something to put on it and a Band-Aid?"

"Sure do, I'll fix him up." Leo responded.

Jake told the sheriff that he would pick Sonny up in the morning, and he would need the cuffs again.

"By the way," Jake asked Leo, "where's Homer? It's strange not seeing him here."

"Homer is working on something he calls stumps..." Leo responded.

Jake decided to go home and clean up so he wouldn't smell like a barnyard when he went to see his lady. Besides, he needed to grab her new cell phone.

Mam smelled her son's fresh Paco as he got ready to leave and she asked him, "Would you like to take some honey biscuits with you for Orpha and the kids? I've got fresh ones made and a jar of honey."

Jake readily agreed, secured them and left – right after he ate two. He was planning on taking Angela to the Little Chico Mexican Eatery for supper, but he would be hungry again by then.

He pulled into her driveway and she come running out as usual and jumped into his arms before he could even get out of the vehicle. Man, he loved this kind of a welcome. It was getting harder and harder to behave himself – but he kept remembering Mam's broom handle.

As they ate their chimichangas, enchilada style, and drank

their raspberry ice tea, they didn't seem to be aware of anyone else in the building. Jake took the little box from his pocket and handed it to her. Excitedly she looked at the picture of the cell phone on the front of the box.

"Open it my lady." Jake told her.

She carefully pulled out the little hot pink cell phone like it might break. "Wow," she exclaimed, "for me?"

"You bet, my soon to be wife. You said you wanted to be able to reach me. Now you can, and you can call Mam. I've programmed Mam's and my cell phone numbers, along with Doc Lowery's, Jani's, Jess's, Dad's and Little Joe's into the phone. All you have to do is push this arrow button until the telephone number comes up you want to call, and then you press this little green telephone button."

"Can I call Mam and give her my number?" She asked.

"Absolutely, just push the arrow button until it says 'Josie Judd' then push the green button and see what happens." He told her.

"Yes!" She shrieked as she pressed on the green send button and waited for someone to answer.

"Hello Angela Honey," Josie answered, "what a pleasant surprise."

"How'd ya know it was me?" She asked Mam.

"The caller ID is a screen that tells me who is calling and it said Angela Crabtree, so I knew it was my little red head. Jake will show you how the caller ID works. I've got your cell number on my Caller ID, and I'll call you back so you can see what it does and hear your new phone ring." Mam told her.

"Yur the first one I called on my new cell, Mam. Now we cain tak." She related to Josie.

Angela hung up and waited for Josie to call back. As the telephone rang, Jake showed her the word 'Josie Judd' in the screen on the front, and how to open it up on its tiny hinges and say hello.

"Wow, it also has Mam's number," Angela said as she started speaking into the telephone – after Jake showed her where to, "Hi, it's me, is that you?" She asked Josie.

"Sure is honey, now you can call me whenever you want to. The best way to answer is to say your name so people will know

if they have dialed a correct number. Just say, 'Angela speaking'.
Then they will know it's you."

"My phone that Jake got me is brite pink, isn't that neat?"
Angela said gleefully.

They talked for a few more minutes. Angela told Mam what
they were having for supper, including how much it costs – and
what booth they were sitting in – on the same side so they could be
touching. Then both ladies got the 'ticklebug' and started laughing
at everything. Josie and Jani sometimes get the ticklebug, like the
yawnbug, but Jake hadn't witnessed Mam getting it with anyone
else.

Jake knew he had hit a winner, that his lady and Mam will
have fun getting better acquainted, and she will be able to get help
in the event of an emergency.   He showed her how to charge the
phone each night, and put it in the little red case to protect it when
she wasn't using it. He had punched a hole in the case and ran a nice
cord through it so she could wear it around her neck. Angela seemed
to be thrilled with everything Jake did. It would also be handy to be
able to call her to see if she could go with him somewhere.

After Angela said good-by to Mam, she started scrolling
again, and then pushed the send button. Jake's cell started ringing.
As he answered it the little voice came,

"Jake Judd, this is Angela Crabtree." He about split a gut,
she was sitting right next to him, but Mam had told her to identify
herself – so she did.

But Jake had to take his lady home; he still had work to
do tonight on his secret project. The idea hit him that Ira might
possibly be willing to help him to speed things up. It was getting so
hard to leave when he took Angela home; he just didn't want to be
without her. She was now part of him.

Next morning he was waiting for Sonny when he actually
showed up on time. There was something about his demeanor
that troubled Jake, but he didn't say anything, he just watched and
listened. Something was in his shirt pocket, but it wasn't a package
of cigarettes. Jake kept completely silent, as he watched Sonny keep

pinching whatever was in his pocket every time the sheriff or Homer said anything. Jake's keen ears were hearing a hum.

"Don't think we'll set too many posts today, I think we'll check out a bit more on Beth's Petting Zoo." Jake finally said to him.

Jake noticed when he started to talk; Sonny would also pinch whatever was in his pocket, and would pinch it again when Jake stopped talking. Plus when Sonny would say something to him he would always start it by saying "Jake." Curious thing Jake thought to himself.

As John came out to greet them, Jake whispered in his ear, "He's recording everything we say. I can hear a slight whine when he pinches his pocket. So say as little as possible."

John nodded and he and Barstow took off talking.

The two fellows went back to the fence and sat four more poles. There were only about four left to finish when Jake told Sonny he wanted to walk over to the area John Stoddard had mentioned for the zoo. Sonny was feeling his shirt pocket, then his jeans pockets, then back to his shirt pocket. The shirt pocket was flat.

"I've dropped something," he told Jake, "I'll be right back, I need to check the work area."

"Sure." Jake agreed and stopped to wait and watch as the young man was frantically looking for whatever he had dropped.

A few moments later he came back to Jake shrugging his shoulders, and they walked on toward the planned zoo location.

Jake started stepping off a possible pen for the little animals as he asked Sonny, "I wonder how much room these little creatures will need. Have you ever been to a petting zoo?"

"Never," was Sonny's response, "don't know anything about them, my folks were always too busy to take me anywhere for fun."

"I'm sorry Sonny; kids need fun and recreation with their parents. Hopefully you can help with the zoo. I think you are afraid of most animals, and I figure it's because you've never been exposed to them. They are really neat little creatures God made for us to enjoy." Jake told him.

"I don't believe in God." Sonny quipped. "Of course you don't; being neglected like you have been," the big man said sympathetically, "but you will get exposed to them here at the ranch and I think you will decide you like them. They are unselfish, and they love you unconditionally. You don't have to do anything but love them back. Some idiots are mean to animals, and the little guys still freely forgive them. It's like God built into them the fact that you have to forgive others before you can get forgiveness. You must also learn to forgive yourself, Sonny, and that's hard."

"Don't preach at me." Sonny snapped. It wasn't until later that he realized Jake had been calling him Sonny - not Sissy.

As Jake dropped Sonny off at the Sheriff's Office, he handed Leo the cuffs telling him he didn't think he would need these anymore. Leo was quite surprised. He also handed the sheriff a small box as he whispered to Leo to give it back to Sonny after about four weeks.

"No one took Wayne again today, Jake," the sheriff was saying, "no one seems to want him around. I always just send him home about ten o'clock. I think he would really like to help someone. He needs companionship."

"See you in the morning, Sonny," Jake told him as he left, "we'll be taking the bike to the City to pick up some Tap-Con nails that Lane Lumber doesn't carry."

The bike? Sonny thought.

After Jake left, Sheriff Leo told the kid that Jake has a big green Gold Wing. Sonny felt a surge of excitement go through him that he had never felt before, and it felt good. He had seen so many motorcycles, but had never been on one. Tomorrow would be exciting.

A Harsh Meeting

Sonny Boatright was at the Sheriff's Office before any of the other boys. He went right to his cell and sat down quietly to wait for the big man with his big bike. When Jake walked in Sonny jumped to his feet and walked up behind him as he said,

"I didn't hear your bike come in."

"Nope, it's quiet." Jake replied. After asking Deputy Homer if he needed anything from the City, he nodded for Sonny to come with him.

The kid's eyes were as big as dollars as he looked at the beautiful green machine.

"I ain't never seen anything so beautiful." He told Jake, who just smiled and nodded.

Jake handed Sonny an older helmet and as the kid put it on his head it was obvious he didn't know how to tighten the chinstrap. Jake started explaining the process to him by showing him on his straps as he held the helmet to his waist to keep it steady. After a few tries Sonny succeeded, and didn't even wait for Jake to tell him to mount the bike. Jake had a bit of a problem getting his chinstrap tightened after he put his helmet on without his helpmeet there to do it for him, but he finally got it tight.

They could talk through the intercom as they rode. Jake could see Sonny's eyes in the rear view mirror. Right now he was just a kid taking his first ride on a big bike, and there wasn't any bully in him.

"We're having an Exchange in the Town Square on the twenty-first, and if you are up to it, I think I'll have the sheriff deputize you so you can be a helper to Deputy Homer. Any thoughts on that?" Jake asks his rider.

"Me? A Deputy? A – Sure I – A - would like to help the deputy – but – me? A Deputy?" The kid kept stammering for words.

He had never even had a thought to keeping the peace – he had always been the one who instigated problems. He kept shaking his head as the thought tried to sink in, that he would be doing something good; that Jake thought he would be a good help to Deputy Homer; that he could do something important.

"Yes." Sonny finally resounded with a nod. He could do something worthwhile.

No one took Wayne again, but instead of Homer letting him go home he told the boy to come and sit down at his desk.

"Wanna tell me what's goin' on?" The deputy asked him.

Wayne waited quite a while before he spoke. The deputy had found the tape recorder and had silently turned it on as he was fiddling with paperwork.

When he broke the silence, Wayne said, "Everyone thinks I got a horrible disease. My dad died 'bout six months ago of Sickle Cell Disease an' a heart attack. They think I got it an' they'll get it from me. Tha's' why I hang with the bigger boys, they ain't afraid of nothin'.'"

Homer was almost speechless, he wasn't used to being a confidant, but he had witnessed Mr. Jake help others, and he wanted to be like the big man.

"I ain't afraid of you Wayne," Deputy Homer assured him, "usually when someone's afraid of something it's because they don't know about it. I don't know much about it, so tell me a little bit."

"It ain't catchable. Yur born with it. It's bad genes that you get from yur mom an' pop, tha's the only way yu can get it. I guess your body don't make enough good cells to keep yur body workin' an' the one's it does make get hard an' funny shaped so they can't get to where they need's to. It really hurts badly; my pappy had lots an' lots of pain. He an' my mommy would cry together as he screamed." Wayne's eyes were full of tears as he added; "Can I go Deputy Homer?"

Homer nodded at the young boy; he was so emotional that he couldn't speak as he realized that the young boy had really been through a horrific time. The deputy was so glad he had taped what the kid was saying, because he couldn't remember parts of it.

That afternoon when Jake and Sonny got back from the City there was a couple sitting in the sheriff's office as they walked in. Sonny went right into his cell and sat down, without speaking to the people.

"Jake," Leo said, "these are Sonny's parents. They are here to register a complaint about how you have been treating their son."

"Gee whiz," Jake quipped, "it only took five days for them to show up."

Wally Boatright stood up as he snarled at Jake, "Do you know who I am?"

"Sure do," remarked Jake, "you're the parents that care a lot more for money than your two kids."

"Sheriff, are you going to let him talk to me like that?" Mr. Boatright said rebukingly to Leo.

But Leo didn't have time to answer because Jake continued, "Sonny is in the process of becoming a man. Since you wouldn't teach him I am taking on the responsibility. One hundred years from now, you will be a pile of dust – so will your money. What will you have taught your children? I think Sonny has worth, a lot more than all your dang money."

"I'm going to sue you Jake Judd. My lawyers will be here this next week for depositions." Mr. Boatright informed Jake.

"Well, if you want to continue to ruin Sonny's life, you go right ahead," Jake informed Wally and Irene, "I still have the upper hand because I have at least two years to file Aggravated Felony attempted Rape charges, along with inciting a riot, and kidnapping - among others. I have a lot of witnesses, and Sonny will go to prison instead of being here with the Sheriff getting rehabilitated by people who actually care what happens to him."

The Boatrights both became very indignant and started raising their voices to Jake, "We know more about the law than you do, Mr.

Judd, and you are in for the fight of your life. You're nothing but a ragged mountain man with no sense."

"It's supposed to be without any sense; you just used a double negative. I graduated with a 4.0 – what was your score?" Jake asked them in a soft voice.

Sonny had been listening very closely from his cell. He finally stood up and broke his silence with,

"Alright you two, Jake's right, you've always cared more for your money and financial condition than me or Donna. If you try to sue Jake, I'll testify for him in court and admit I'm guilty."

The Boatrights were floored, "But we thought you wanted to get away from here."

"I did, but not to prison. Besides, I might be worth something after all," Sonny hollered at them, "in fact, if the sheriff will OK it, I'm going to be a Special Deputy to help Deputy Homer at the Exchange on the twenty-first."

"Why are you acting like this?" They asked their son.

"Because Jake's right, you've never cared what happened to me or my sister. We're just bothers and time wasters to you. All you ever care about is your money. Well, you can take your money and put it where the sun don't shine – I don't care." Sonny retaliated.

"Easy boy," Jake said softly to Sonny, "they are still your parents and the Bible says you have to treat them with respect even when they don't deserve it."

Sonny sat back down in his cell as his parents glared at both Sheriff Leo and at Jake who remained quiet. After about five minutes of silence, the Boatrights got up and walked out mumbling to each other.

"You know the cell door isn't locked." Jake said to Sonny after they left. "I know." Sonny replied softly.

"Sheriff and Mr. Jake, I got somethin' for you to listen to, and I guess it's all right for Sonny to listen too." Homer said to delay anyone leaving. But, I'll have to tell Sonny I got something of his."

The deputy looked at Jake and then at the Sheriff. They both nodded their approval of telling Sonny that they have his tape deck. As the four men sat down around Homer's desk –he took the recorder out of it. Sonny looked at Jake, who just raised his eyebrows as he ginned at the young man.

"No one wanted Wayne again, so I asked him some questions, and remembered Sonny's recorder so I wouldn't forget what he said. Here's what the little boy said." The deputy stated as he pushed play on Sonny's recorder.

As Wayne's shaking voice told the story of his father's horrible death, neither man could say anything, not even Sonny. Sonny had never felt these kinds of emotions before, nor had he really stopped to think about what someone other than himself had gone through. As Jake watched Sonny's heart soften, he knew the Lord was working on this roughian of a young man.

"Here's your recorder back Sonny," Sheriff Leo finally said as he broke the silence, "but I am going to keep the tape, and I'll buy you a new one."

Sonny nodded as he said, "I can get it later, and you might need to listen to the tape again. I'll be around."

"Come on, let's get something to eat," Jake said to Sonny and nodded at Deputy Homer to see if he would like to join them.

The three men left for McDonald's. Deputy Homer kept Sonny between himself and Mr. Jake and sat on the kid's side of the table.

As they ate, Jake was talking to Deputy Homer about having Sonny be his Special Deputy to help keep the peace at the Exchange. Homer readily agreed as long as it was all right with the sheriff. Deputy Homer told Sonny that he would discuss it with Sheriff Leo and let him know.

Sonny was excitedly telling Homer about the big bike ride; and how quiet – it – was….ooops – he remembered Homer's noisy Harley – and was sure he had blown his chances of being a special deputy…But Homer graciously ignored the 'noisy' comment.

It felt so good to be talking 'right' conversation with people, not defensive aggressive talk, but grown up talk. He was becoming a 'man'.

The mountain man was again thinking how very lucky he is to have parents that cared enough to train and teach him.

Suddenly Homer went into orbit. Jake turned to see what Homer was staring at and he saw his little sister sitting at the booth across the room with her friend Elaine Caldwell. Jani was coy at first, but finally smiled back at Homer as she stared back.

As the three men left the restaurant, Homer passed close to Jani's table and tipped his hat at her. Jake thought she seemed giddy.

Sonny headed for the Rainrest Motel as Jake and Homer headed for the Post Office. Ira was also walking to his Post Office Box for his mail so he joined Jake and Homer. The deputy felt small following the two big men, but he would get back on his stumps as soon as he got home.

"Howdy Bro." Jake said to Ira.

"Howdy Bro." Ira returned the greeting.

"Did John Stoddard get a hold of Todd? He wants to ask him some questions on drafting." Jake asked Ira.

"Yea," Ira responded, "Todd's going out tomorrow to see what John has in mind. By the way, how are you coming on your secret project?"

"Slow," Jake answered, "it's hard with only one arm."

"How about some help Jake?" Ira asked.

"That would be great," Jake confirmed, "the faster I get it done the sooner we can get married."

"I'll go home with you now and we can work this evening if you're up to it." Ira responded as he picked a small white envelope out of his pile of mail, and tried non-chalantly to open it. He casually sniffed the envelope - and as he pulled the card out of it – he started grinning. The little card had pretty flowers all over the front of it.

"What's that?" Jake asked grinning back.

"Nothing – just a thank you note." Ira answered.

"Who from, to make you grin like a rooster?" Jake inquired.

"Roosters don't grin," Ira reminded Jake, "but it's a note from Leslie thanking me for helping with the little girl's rescue. She says she is proud of me…No one's ever told that to me before."

Ira put the pretty little card in his shirt pocket and a small bit of the card stuck out of the pocket showing the edges of the pretty flowers.

Ordinarily, Jake thought to himself, *a man might get teased with flowers sticking out of his pocket, but I doubt that Ira will have that problem.*

The three men walked back to the Sheriff's Office. Jake and Ira jumped in the ATV and headed for the mountain to work on the special project. Homer headed for home on his noisy bike.

Three hours later as the two men entered the kitchen, Mam already had the table set for dinner, and there was an extra plate for Ira.

"How'd you know I'd be here?" Ira asked Mam.

"Spies." Mam answered smiling.

Everyone sat down and Dad said grace. Then everyone dived in. Uncle Ernie had been working on his hydrogen project all day, and he and Little Joe were hyped up about it.

Unc was saying, "Existing automobiles could be economically converted to burn Hydrogen fuel, and I think it will even reverse the Greenhouse Effect. Now, you saw how the flame went up when I lit that little tube Joe, right?"

"I did." Agreed Joe.

Unc continued before Joe could say any thing else, "So you see how Hydrogen can even be stored and managed through the natural gas systems we already have in place across the entire country. This would make it available to everyone."

Uncle Ernie and Joe were so deep in conversation about the possibility of ballast's controlling any possible explosions that they finished their meals without tasting them and headed back to their Third Level, forgetting to say their adieu's to anyone. The family started laughing as the two came back in briefly to pick up their dishes, rinse them and put them in the dishwasher, then head back up stairs without wavering in their discussion. The pair is always good to call out the ticklebug.

Hole in the Wall Gang

After dinner Jake and Ira went back to work. They were loading the Evacuation Drum with their diggings.

Mam was in the kitchen when all of a sudden 'crash'; a hole appeared in the wall with a whole bunch of laughter coming from behind it.

Jake poked his head through as he said, "Howdy."

Mam started laughing too. As they enlarged the hole, carefully so they wouldn't stir up too much more dust than they already had, it was apparent that Jake had been putting a lot of work into a tunnel he had been digging out. It needed some smoothing up and some type of covering on the walls, but they could stand up in it. He had lumber stacked along the wall to firm up the walls and attach the plywood to. He was taking Dads' example of using three-quarter plywood for walls, ceilings and floors for under-sheathing. It was a really strong base for attaching finishing products to.

"Figured we'd need a way to get to the kitchen without going through the basement." Jake said as the two men were cracking up.

"Yea," Ira responded "must always be a way to Mam's kitchen, especially when your wife can't cook."

That cracked both of them up again, along with Mam. Dad had heard the crash and come running, as did Jani and Jess. The two men were really a sight; they looked like a couple of animals trying to escape from a cage, and just about as dirty. Mam was sure glad Jake had his cast covered!

"You both realize you have to clean up the mess you made in my kitchen." Josie said to them between her cackles.

"Yes Mam." Come the reply from both at the same time.

As Jake and Ira started back to work the rest of the family, even Unc, had joined them, and were all chipping at the mud, rock and clay. Dad grabbed a large floor fan and was blowing the dust down the hallway away from the kitchen – and their nostrils. Of course Uncle Ernie had his lab coat and mesh hat on.

As Mam worked she wasn't chipping much, but was moving down the hall, she wanted to see what was at the end of the hallway. Jani was right behind her.

Jake started giggling again. It was really fun to have help, which meant he could marry his beloved just that much faster.

"Like Mam always says," Jake said to Ira, "a sorrow shared is only half a sorrow, but a joy shared is twice the joy."

Most of the apartment was in decent shape, under all the dust. Jake had hollowed out the walls and covered most of them with the elbram from Joe's machine over the plywood. He had attached white elbram to the ceilings that gave the rooms' height and lightness. The rooms really were very striking. The area for the kitchen was just bare elbram walls with a touch of mint green. He had made a nice sized bathroom – with a shower big enough for two. The bedroom would accommodate a king-size bed, which is a must for him. A nice little living room completed the three-room home.

"Later," Jake added, "we'll have to add a nursery – or two. I've got the drains drilled down to the lower level, and I have to see how Unc and Joe want them connected to the recycle system. Hopefully we can get that done next weekend along with the carpet in the bedroom and living room, their sub-flooring is ready. I want Angela to help me pick out the carpet colors. I'm working on the ivory elbram for the kitchen floor right now – much to Joe's dismay. He sure gets grouchy with me running the machine all night."

Mam was pleased to see that there was a hole in the living room wall for a picture window that looked over the valley on the far side of the mountain. Jake had to get the window along with a door to put in the wall yet, but otherwise the living room was almost done.

There was a big flat rock outside of the living room area that he was turning into a patio. The view from the patio was fantastic.

The lake almost looked like a heart, and the trees were reaching up to their Creator.

"I have to put up a good fence around the patio for safety for…" Jake paused, then added, "Dad is working on the iron right now."

"For our grandchildren," Mam popped up; "they have to be safe from falling."

Jake's smile was now pushing his ears back as he continued, "We have to look at kitchen cabinets and appliances, and some living room furniture. Of course I'm going to take Angela with me to pick out her new furnishings and we'll need to borrow your Jimmy, Dad. The water lines are all in place; they just have to be connected at the other end. I'm hoping to do that this weekend. "

Jake had put many months into his project, and it was coming together very nicely.

"Oh, and we have to get a bed set." He said sheepishly.

Mam and Dad had known all along what their son was doing, as did the rest of the family. It was fun being included now, and Mam couldn't wait for Angela to see her new home. Josie also noticed a little plastic table in the living room now held the golden sack.

"What about a closet?" Jani asked.

Jake paused…"Whoops, I guess I'd better get one done." Her big brother responded embarrassedly to his oversight.

"With the hallway down into the garage, we won't have to bother anyone when we're coming or going and Angela can get to the utility room with laundry." He told his family, "This other hall isn't as long because it goes straight down to the garage and Unc's gardens go under some of our new home. We will have to go through the gardens to get upstairs, but that's sure OK.

Oh, and Jess, when I pick up the furniture I'd like you to go with me to help carry and load it." Jake said to his little brother.

"Absolutely," Jess answered.

"I can help too," Ira chimed in.

"Angela and I will go and pick everything out and pay for it tomorrow, and you fellas can all go in a couple of days to bring it home." Jake had planned it all out; he wanted to be alone with his soon to be wife to pick out their furniture.

They were all getting caught up in the excitement when Mam's phone rang, "Hello Mam," the soft little voice at the other end spoke, "this is Angela Crabtree."

"Hi Honey," Mam answered grinning at how she identified herself again, "we were just talking about you and how excited we all are that you are joining our family. Jake said he's going to take you shopping, sounds like fun." Mam didn't tell her for what or about the apartment - that was for Jake to do.

After Mam hung up, Jake called his lady, "Hi my love, does Kelli work tomorrow, or can she sit with your mother while we go to the City?"

"I'll ask 'er then I'll call ya back," Angela responded, forgetting to say goodbye.

A few moments later Jakes phone rang again, "Hi Jake Judd, this is Angela Crabtree," Jake started giggling as she introduced herself, "Kelli said fine, she don' work at the 'Do Over' tomorrow, 'cause she works on Saturday this week."

"Great sweetheart, we'll be taking Dad's truck and I'll pick you up about seven thirty in the morning at the road," Jake relayed to her, "Dad will take my ATV to work. I can't wait to see you, I've got a surprise that's ready for you to see before we head to the City."

"I luv yur surpris's," she told her man, "an' I jus' luv yu too."

The starry eyed Jake told his family that when he brings his soon to be wife home in the morning, he would like privacy. They all agreed as Mam squeezed Dad's hand with a knowing squeeze, and he kissed her forehead.

A Proposal

The beautiful little red head was waiting at the corner for her man as Jake pulled up in Dad's GMC. She jumped in and scooted over almost on top of Jake as they kissed an extended hello. She had on a pretty pink 'sissy blouse' and blue jeans. Jake loves his lady in pink, even with her red hair; it makes her look absolutely lovely. Both of their hearts were pounding so hard that they were sure their mate could hear theirs beat. Jake could see the bulge under his love's blouse, and knew she had the gold sack with her.

Jake asked Angela to push the code into the buttons and she remembered them. As she did, the big rock slid back and she leaned forward as if to help the truck get in faster before the rock could close. As the elevator was going down the lovers were making up for lost time kissing. Neither one of them could keep their hands off each other. Jake had to keep remembering to behave toward his lady, and wondered if she was having trouble behaving too. Her kisses were long and sweet.

When they came back to reality they realized the elevator had stopped and they were in the garage. Jake pulled the truck off the elevator and parked it. He went around to Angela's side and opened the door. As she started to climb out he picked her up and held her close to him as he kissed her softly. He took her hand as he lowered her to the floor and they walked through the garden, where she saw steps going up to somewhere. As he led her up the stairs she was getting giggly. He started giggling too. Then he suddenly scooped her up in his right arm and stepped on the top step.

Angela couldn't believe her eyes. "Welcome home, my beautiful helpmeet." Jake whispered to her as he brushed her hair with his lips.

"Oh my gooness," was all she could say, "Oh my gooness."

He sat her down and she started investigating the rooms. When they stepped into the bathroom Jake remarked, "That's a two person shower."

"Sure is, an' it's beautiful." She cooed.

She ran her fingers around the walls and woodwork. Then she walked to the patio as Jake told her,

"I'm going to put a good fence around so the kids won't fall off."

"Good idea," She was still cooing.

"Look around and we'll write down some colors you want to finish our home in." Jake told her.

"Our home, our home," she repeated, "oh Jakie, it's the mostus beautiful thin I ever seen." She started to cry with happiness.

They just stood in their home holding each other closely as their love made a deeper covenant bond.

Jake walked over to the little plastic table and picked up the sack. He took out the little blue velvet box and opened it. Then he got down on one knee as he said amid his tears of joy, "Angela, I love you with all my heart, will you be my wife? Will you accept this ring as a token of my forever love?"

"Yes, yes," She giggled at him as she jumped at him knocking him over. They were both on the floor, as he took the ring out of the box and placed it on the third finger of her left hand. She looked at it briefly, and then their lips met as they each kissed their covenant partner.

He took the chain out of the gold sack after they could finally back off from each other enough to use his hand. Jake took the second ring in her set and put it on the chain and asked her to fasten the chain around his neck as he said, "This is where your ring will stay until I have the honor of placing it on your finger when the pastor pronounces us man and wife."

Now Angela knew what the chains were for, and she took out the sack she had been wearing close to her heart since they purchased the rings, and took out the velvet boxes. As she took out Jakes ring and the chain, she put his ring on her chain, and he fastened the chain around her neck.

"This is where yur ring will stay until I ave tha honor of placin it on yur finger when tha pastor says we ar man an' wife." Angela whispered to him.

They were now officially engaged.

Jake broke the silence and the romance by saying, "We need to concentrate on what colors you want in our home my lady."

He took out a small spiral notebook and they began discussing colors for carpeting, kitchen appliances, living room furniture, and the bedroom. As the bedroom came up, they both giggled.

Angela wanted to show the ring to Mam before anyone else saw it, so they started down the hallway to Mam's kitchen. Mam was waiting at the table with baited breath as they stepped into the kitchen with Angela staring at her finger.

"I wan' ya ta see it first, Mam." Angela said to Josie.

"Oh honey, it's the prettiest ring I've ever seen," her new mother-in-law said to her, "I'm so happy for you and for us. Have you set a date yet?"

"No not yet, but soon." Jake cut in.

Back on the road Angela couldn't keep her eyes off her new ring or her hands off her man. She would pull Jake's ring out where she could see it on the chain, and compare it to hers, as she wiggled around. She was so bubbly she couldn't sit still. Jake put her to work writing things down that they needed to check on, including the carpeting. Since she couldn't write very well, her doodles were like hieroglyphics as she wrote down a refrigerator, a stove, a sofa and chair and even a hamper for their dirty clothes.

"I'll be washin' yur clothes." Angela told him happily.

Jake knew lots of women would call it a nasty chore, but his lady was looking forward to doing his dirty laundry.

"We'll prob'ly hav ta eat with Mam 'til she teaches me ta cook. At home I jus' fix stews and a samwich' or hot dogs." She said it like that might not be a good thing.

"Mam will love that." Jake assured her.

"We're gettin' married, we're gettin' married" Angela started singing, and soon her betrothed joined her.

They visited the carpet store first, and picked out what they wanted, silver blue for the living room and emerald green for the bedroom. Jake asked the salesman to have the carpet loaded in the GMC.

Next was the furniture store where they picked out a dark blue print sofa with ivory flowers and green leaves and a matching chair. They found two perfect brass looking lamps with ivory octagon shades; oak end tables and coffee table with brass looking inserts rimming the glass embedded in the top; along with a really cute oval kitchen dinette set that had a 'parquet' looking top and four tan chairs with wheels.

"Wow, it's so fancy." Angela kept saying about everything.

They would take the lamps with them now because she could carry one and Jake the other.

Jake knew they wouldn't be able to get much in the truck with the carpeting being so bulky and heavy, and he wanted to get that home first to put in this weekend. So he paid for what they picked out and scheduled the pick up for a couple of day's later. Ira offered his pick up, but Jake wasn't sure it would make the mountain path. However, he could drive to the turn around and they could re-load it into the GMC to take it the rest of the way. Ira said that Todd and Billy wanted to help too. Sonny also asked if he could be included in the 'festivities'. Sounded like a workable plan. Including Jess, the six staunch men could certainly handle the situation, and it would give Todd the opportunity to see that Sonny was growing into a decent man.

Next came the refrigerator, stove – and a dishwasher. Angela had fallen in love with a dishwasher, but she couldn't figure how she was to cook on that flat stove, it had no burners on top of it for the fire to come out. It was just plain strange. Jake told her the stove is called a ceramic top, and showed her how the rings were laid out on the stove, and that they get hot for cooking. Their new home was all solar electric so they didn't have anything that was gas. The refrigerator had an icemaker in the top of it, and Angela couldn't figure out how the thing could make ice in the hot summer. Their little frig at home couldn't even keep the food cold in the summers, let alone make ice.

Jake decided that Angela and Jani should do the shopping for the sheets, towels and any other linen they would need. That sounded good to his little red head, she and Jani wanted to spend some time together anyway.

They found some really pretty pre-made oak cabinets for the kitchen and the store could order the countertop to fit any size of the lower cabinets they bought. They decided on a blue metallic countertop that would blend nicely with the ivory floor and the living room carpet. The oak bathroom cabinet matched the kitchen cabinets, and this thrilled Angela. The bathroom sink top was one piece gold streaked marble with holes in it, and room on each side to put things. Angela couldn't figure out how water would stay in the sink, but Jake assured her he would be putting a faucet in the top holes and a drain in the hole in the bottom of the sink. They got a double kitchen sink to match the almond stove; refrigerator and dishwasher with pretty chrome faucets - with a sprayer. Angela had never seen a sink sprayer before and it looked fun.

Jake wondered how many times she would flood the kitchen before she mastered the sprayer.

Next was the bedroom furniture. Seemingly a bit embarrassed about trying out a bed in front of the salesman, Jake asked the salesman, "Will you please give us some privacy?"

The salesman disappeared.

They were alone with bedroom furniture. They kept giving each other silly looks as they tried out different mattresses. They kept returning to the one 'pillow top', it was really soft and comfortable, and it had a satin covering on it that was 'really fancy' according to Angela. It did have a firm support, however, so it would be good for their backs. They agreed on the 'fancy' one.

They spotted an oak bedroom suite that would match their cabinets, and they both loved it. There were scrolls on the doors that the handles fit into, and feet with toes on the bottom. Angela kept laughing at dressers having toes,

"Do we nail polish them?" She giggled.

They took a chest of drawers, a dresser with a mirror, the

headboard and footboard that matched, along with the rails that hooked the two ends together and held the mattress and box springs off the floor. The head and footboards even had toes on the ball feet.

They found the perfect hamper. It was gold to match the grain in the bathroom countertop and it would go home with them today.

Angela was still giggling when Jake paid for everything, "feet on ar bed, I hope it don' run aroun' all nite."

The salesman grinned at Jake as the big man turned red.

Jake knew they would need more things, but after they bought a white rattan settee with two matching chairs and coffee table, they were done for the day. He really needed to get the patio ready for the furniture, which will be such a romantic place to enjoy their evenings together looking over the big valley from the eagles view.

After getting something to eat they headed for home. Angela was tired, and before too long she was snoozing with her head on Jake's shoulder. He kept kissing the top of his woman's head. He was overwhelmed with gratitude that the Good Lord had given him such a special woman. He was truly grateful that they had both saved themselves for their mates.

He knows from now until the wedding it will be even harder to keep themselves in check, but that's God's way, and he want's God's blessings on his marriage.

God cannot look on sin, and I want Him in our marriage. The mountain man was thinking as he drove.

With the carpet sticking out the back of the GMC they received some looks from the town folk. Most of them knew what was going on; Jake and Angela had been together for over a year, and they figured a marriage was in the makings.

After a long goodbye, Jake dropped his beloved off at the corner because she had to relieve Kelli. Then he called Jess and asked him to meet him in the garage and help him take the carpet up to the apartment. Jess told him Ira was there waiting also.

Deputy Homer's Investigation

Homer couldn't sleep, he kept tossing and turning in his bed, thinking how uninformed people are on Sickle Cell Disease, and that makes them afraid of people with SCD. He had also been afraid of people with this dastardly disease - they had been born with.

"They didn't do anythin' wrong, they were born with it," he kept saying out loud to himself, "I didn't know either. I need to know more. I'm a deputy, and it's my job to protect people, 'specially ones with terrible diseases."

Finally, since he couldn't sleep, he decided to go to the office and get on the sheriff's computer and check out something he had heard about called webmd.com and see if he could learn more about Sickle Cell.

As he sat down and booted up the computer he decided to start the recorder too so he could put important information into it.

He learned that Sickle Cell Disease is truly inherited. It cannot be caught from anyone. It causes something called red blood cells to be deformed. They turn into what looks like a curved boomerang – or sickle – shape, and they can't get through the blood veins with oxygen to keep the body working. Homer learned that your red blood cells carry oxygen all over your body. And when your body doesn't get the oxygen it needs it becomes very very painful.

These sickle cells get hard, and they clog up the arteries. After the oxygen escapes from the red blood cells, the remainder of the cells clump together and cause heart attacks. The red cells on a healthy person live about 120 days, but the red cells of the victims of this disease only live about 20 days, and their weak bodies can't replace the dead ones fast enough, so they have to have transfusions all of the time.

The young deputy wasn't sure he was saying things correctly into the recorder, and he couldn't pronounce some of the big words, like c-h-r-o-m-o-s-o-m-e-s, but the sheriff could. He also saw the words 'autosomal recessive disease' he couldn't say, but he would print the information off the web. It says that to have the disease a baby has to get a gene for the disease from each parent. It has to have two of these genes to have the disease. Some people have something called a trait, but not the disease, even though if they marry someone who also has the trait, their children will have sickle cell disease.

Man, Homer thought, *this medical stuff is amazing. Jani wants to be a doctor and she has to learn all this. Doc Lowery should know about this sickle cell stuff.*

Homer spelled into the tape, "It says there are two kinds of h-e-m-o-g-l-o-b-i-n, an A and an S. The people with the A's are just carriers. But it's bad when both parents have the S because they have the disease and will give it to their babies. I wonder if Wayne and his younger brother, Wilson, have had this here simple test called 'High-Performance Liquid C-h-r-o-m-a-t-o-g-r-a-p-h-y or HPLC for short? I wonder if their mom has been checked. 'Course that don't matter 'cause they are already born."

There was a flag for the drugs they use to treat the disease.

"Wow," he said right out loud as he clicked on the flags, "the treatment will cause death and severe side effects. This H-y-d-r-o-x-y-u-r-e-a – oral - sounds like it's worse than the disease. It's also very expensive and it says you have to wear throwaway gloves when touching it. Man, no one could hardly work with this disease and all the pain. Gosh, we should always be nice and gentle with anyone with Sickle Cell Disease. They need someone to care about them – not be mean to them."

"Gosh," Homer continued talking out loud to himself, "I always thought only black people got the disease, but it says here that 1 in 400 Black babies have it, 1 in 1,000 Hispanic babies have it and 1 in

50,000 White babies have it. One in twelve Black people carry the 'traits' and don't have the actual disease."

As the tired deputy turned off the recorder about three a.m. and shut down the computer, he lay his head down on his desk for only a moment – he was so tired. He thought he would rest a few moments, then get back on his Computer English Lessons.

About Six a.m. Sheriff Leo walked in and found him slumped over his desk.

"Homer, you all right?" Leo asked with concern.

Raising his head as he shook it back and forth, the deputy realized he had slept for about three hours as he answered, "Yea, sheriff, I'm all right. I just couldn' sleep so I got on the computer to check out this horrible disease Mr. Close died from. Do you want to listen to what I put on the tape?"

"Sure." Leo agreed.

As they were listening to it Sonny walked in early again. He stood listening also. Although he hadn't heard the entire message, he had a suggestion,

"Sheriff, what do you think about playing this for all six of us fella's when they get here?"

Leo looked at Sonny a moment and then replied, "Sonny, what an excellent idea. You are so right on. We'll have Jake listen too."

Sonny nodded, he felt good because he had an idea, and others thought was good.

As the nine men listened they were totally focused. Homer had put it back to the beginning where Wayne was telling his story and then the explanation followed. Wayne was a bit embarrassed at first with everyone hearing his story, but as Max and Ronnie put their arms around his shoulders, he felt like maybe something good was going to happen.

"Sheriff," Homer was saying when the tape finished, "I want to take this over and let Doc listen to it, and then Barstow. Is that OK?"

The choked up sheriff nodded yes.

"Good work, Deputy Homer," Jake said to him, "I'm proud of you."

Doc Lowery was sitting behind his desk when Homer walked in.

"Mornin' Doc," Homer greeted him, "I've got something for you to listen to. It's about the Close family."

Doc Lowery nodded at the deputy to start the tape as he stopped the paperwork he was doing and focused on the recorder Homer had in his hand. As the tape finished both men were silent for a while. Doc was letting everything sink in.

Doc finally broke the silence with, "Sickle Cell Disease is a horrible scourge on its victims. I've known about it for many years, but I've never really been involved with it. I think it's good, Homer, that you are bringing it to light. People are afraid of what they don't know. So you don't know if either boy or their mother have been tested?"

"From what Wayne said, neither one have been tested, they can't afford it," Homer answered, "but Doc, if yu'll do that HPLC test on 'em, I'll figure out a way to pay ya – maybe ya can take payments?"

Doc just smiled at the concerned deputy, "well right now, Homer, the money isn't a consideration, let's just get them tested. How do you purpose to get them here?"

The deputy thought for a few moments before he spoke, "Well, it won't be a problem to git Wayne here cause he's under our control. But I don't know 'bout his mom or brother Wilson."

"We can start with Wayne, if he doesn't have both S-genes, then chances are Wilson won't either," Doc told him, "so how soon can you get Wayne here with his mom's signature on this Permission Authorization since he is only fourteen."

Homer hadn't thought about needing permission from his mom. "Give me the paper, and I'll give it to Wayne in the morning to take home with him. Now I'm going to go see Barstow." Homer informed the Doc.

But as he was speaking Barstow Perez walked into the Doc's office asking, "Deputy Homer, I understand you want to talk to me about young Wayne Close. What's up?"

Homer rewound the tape and played it for Barstow from the beginning. The large man was obviously deeply touched as he said,

"Homer, this is a good thing you are doing. This is some outstanding work getting Wayne's story on the tape, then going onto the computer to check it out. I'm proud of you."

The young deputy was reeling from being told twice in only one day that someone was proud of him, first Jake then Barstow, both powerful decent men.

"I'm fully aware of what causes this disease. My wife and I have always told everyone Mia is barren. But that's not quite the whole story. We both have the Sickle Cell Disease Trait, and we decided as soon as we found out that we would not have children to pass this terrible disease on to. Instead, God blessed us with letting us be involved with John Stoddard's kids and grandkids. I guess it's time the truth came out. Doc has known all along and thank you Dr. Lowery for your protecting our secret."

Barstow told them both through the tears of relief he was releasing; partly because of the hurt; but mostly because he and his wife didn't have to lie anymore. John and Emily had been aware right from the beginning, and had never been afraid of them.

"After all this family has been through in the grip of the disease, and hands of uninformed people, I think it would behoove our town if John would tell the facts about this disease from the pulpit Sunday morning, or even let me speak on it." Barstow said with conviction, "I don't have the actual disease, but I can certainly speak on what it is, unless you would like to talk on the subject, Deputy, since you are the one who did all the work finding out about it."

"No, no, Mr. Barstow, you do it." Homer commented.

A Ramp & Ranch Visit

As Jake and Sonny left for their day's work Jake headed toward the West Side of town. He pulled into Lane Lumber. Sonny didn't care where they were going, he was actually glad to be working with this big man today. Not much was said, but he did introduce Sonny to Harvey, who just nodded as Jake gave him the list of supplies he needed.

Sonny jumped out of the ATV and started helping the two men load the lumber on the roll bars and put the Quik Crete in the rumble seat. There was a black drum about eighteen inches tall with a green lid. The sides had big grooves in them. The kid didn't have any idea what it was for, but he knew he'd be finding out. There was also a plain white five-gallon bucket with a metal handle that had a wooden spool on it, which was filled with an assortment of hammers, nails, screwdrivers and saws and some funny looking flat steel paddles with wooden handles. One of the flat paddles had one edge that turned up about half an inch. A steel tape hung on Jake's belt that had 24' on the label attached to it. Sonny started getting hyper; they were going to build something, what a trip.

As they pulled up into Angela's driveway, here she came and landed right on top of the big man before he could even get out of the vehicle. Sonny's eyes were staring in amazement as they kissed and she held her hand out to show their guest her new ring.

Jake pried her off of him as he introduced Sonny to her. Sonny waited to see if she was going to jump him like she did Jake, but she held her hand out to shake his as she told him,

"I'm Jake's soon to be wife, Angela. Pleaz ta meet ya Sonny."

He was relieved – although somewhat jealous – that he didn't have to pry her off of himself.

Jake started digging down on the outside of the forms they had nailed together. He dug until the outside of the form was even with the ground and the side closest to the house was the three and one half inches of the two by four above the ground.

"That'll make a nice smooth entrance for the chair," he told Sonny, "now please get me the black container with the green lid and we'll mix some concrete. I'll need the five gallon bucket emptied and filled with water from the spigot there at the end of the house."

As Sonny picked up the black container he looked at it – So this is a hand cement mixer, but it's going to be heavy to shake. He thought to himself.

Jake put part of a bag of concrete mix in the black container, then added some water and put the lid on it. He tipped it over sideways, and started rolling it around with his foot.

"Whew," came a sigh of relief from the kid, "I don't have to lift it."

Jake snickered.

Sonny had watched very carefully how much concrete mix and water Jake had put into the black bucket. So Sonny stepped up to roll the black container with his foot so Jake could do whatever else he could when he saw the most beautiful girl he had ever laid eyes on. He also saw the big man watching, so he kept on working, but his foot kept slipping off the bucket because his eyes couldn't stay on it.

Jake sighed, "Like Homer when Jani passes, they go bonkers."

"I think that's mixed enough, Sonny," Jake was saying to the young man, who finally heard him and bounced back to reality, "I'll empty it into the forms and you can start a second batch.

Angela had stepped up beside the young lady as she introduced the two, "Pam, this is Sonny, and Sonny this is Pam."

Sonny wasn't sure what to do with a lady; most of the girls he dated were not ladies, so he just bowed. Jake's hand went over his mouth to conceal the humor of it.

"Pam is my bestus friend's Kelli's little sister, well Kelli was my bestus friend, now Jake's my bestus friend, so she's my secon' bestus friend's sister, we all been neighbors since before we's born 'caus' our mom's were bestus friends too."

Sonny had to maul over what Jake's soon to be wife had said before it actually sunk in and he couldn't think of anything to say but, "That's neat."

Jake's chest was still bouncing with chuckles as Angela said she'd walk her former bestus friend's, now second bestus friend's little sister home now. Angela was aware of Sonny's history.

The concrete sat up fast, and by the time is was ready to hold some weight the two men had cut the redwood into four foot pieces for the floor frame, and the four by fours for the pillars into the graduated sizes Jake needed. Sonny was learning to use a level, a square, a hammer and even a power saw, and he now knew what Tap-Con cement nails were for.

He was having a ball as he noted to Jake, "Work can be fun. This is really fun."

The big man smiled as he agreed.

The ramp was ready for try out. Angela and Orpha had been watching from the porch.

"OK Sonny, wheel the chair down the ramp, let's initiate it." Jake told his beaming co-worker.

The young man walked up the ramp and took the handles of the chair and started slowly down the ramp. Orpha's right arm was going frantic.

"Is she OK?" Sonny asked Jake.

"Sure is, she's just excited, Sonny," Jake assured him, "she's been confined to her small home without any way to get out. This will give her some freedom; someone can wheel her down the ramp and take her for a ride around the forest. I've got to figure out some new wheels that will go over the ground better. Now let's head to the ranch and see if Todd made it there yet."

Sonny pushed Orpha's chair back up the ramp, and after Jake's long goodbye with Angela, they were headed toward Stoddards.

"No one's ever welcomed me like that," The young man was saying, "How'd you find Angela?"

"The Lord brought us together. We've been seeing each other for over a year, and I just gave her a ring a week ago. I had to fix us up an apartment first. It's almost done, so it was time to propose." Jake answered.

"Where do you get alone when you want to get sexy?" Sonny inquired.

Instead of smacking the young man into early eternity he decided this was a good time to approach right and wrong with the ladies as he said, "Sonny, Angela and I are both pure, neither of us have had sex before. We're saving it for the marriage bed, like the Bible says we should."

Shocked Sonny asked, "You mean YOU have never been with a woman - you look like a rough man?"

"Looks can be deceiving, Son, but Angela is worth waiting for. You know the old saying 'men shack up with whores, but they marry virgins'? And being a real man isn't measured by conquests." Jake informed him.

"Yea, I've heard the phrase, but I've not been around any good girls, except to conquer them." The young man communicated honestly.

Jake waited a few seconds before he continued, "Sonny, it takes a real man to be able to keep himself in tact. The man is more responsible for the relationship than the women because ladies think with their hearts. You cannot have a special person until you are ready to put her feelings and needs before your own. I want to keep her pure because it is the right thing to do. I will not disrespect her, or cause her to disrespect herself. Sometimes it is hard to behave when my little red head clutches me, but I know it's God's way to treat a lady - with respect."

"There you go with that God talk again." Sonny responded.

"Yes, Sonny, I want to please God so he will bless my marriage," the big man continued, "I know I never have to worry about her stabbing me in the back, or leaving when someone better comes around. She knows the same about me. That's what creates this bond that you can see. I treat her like the lady she is, and she is the lady I want to be my eternal helpmeet."

Sonny was silent as they drove into the ranch, but the wheels were turning loudly in his head.

John, Barstow and Todd were standing there talking. Todd

recognized Sonny as the leader of the roughians and bristled.

"It's OK, Todd," Sonny is becoming a man and helping me do good jobs" Jake told Todd, "got anything decided yet on the zoo?"

"We're still kicking things around, I think I'm getting a pretty good idea of what Mr. Stoddard wants," Todd told Jake, "I'm going to go home and play with these measurements I took. Now I've got to go check to see if Kelli has talked with Mr. Bloom yet and got things set for the twenty-first."

"Kelli, that's Pam's big sister and…." Sonny didn't get to finish his sentence because it was interrupted as Jake stopped Todd in mid air shouting at the young man, "If you touch Pam I'll literally break your neck."

"He won't, Todd, he knows he'd be a dead man if he would even try." Jake assured Todd as he headed for his old Toyota.

Jake looked at Sonny who was trembling as he spoke; "Man if you hadn't been here I'd be dead - at least all broken up."

"We take women-hood very seriously here in the mountains, Sonny," the big man notified him, "we might look like backward dummkopfs, but we know what's right, it's a Mountain Man thing."

"By the way Barstow," Jake continued, "Deputy Homer wants to talk to you, he's got a young man that has burned right into his heart and your wisdom and knowledge may be able to go a long way."

"You bet, Jake," Barstow answered, "I'll call him right away. I'm guessing it's about the young man Homer was telling me about at Doc Lowery's."

"I think he wants to discuss more than the young man." Jake replied.

"Does everyone around just stop what they are doing to help someone else?" Sonny quipped.

"Yep, the Bible says we are to help one another." Jake answered as the young man just rolled his eyes at the mention of God again.

On the way back to the Sheriff's Office Sonny only said one thing, "Is Todd a virgin too?"

"Reckon so, he's a real Mountain Man." Jake affirmed.

Homer Propositions Barstow

Deputy Homer was at the computer checking more things out when Barstow walked in. He noted Wayne was alone in the cell with the door unlocked.

"No one took Wayne today either?" He asked the deputy.

"Nope." Homer replied.

"Well," Barstow continued, "my wife wants the windows washed on our home, do you suppose he's up to helping me?"

"Yes!" Came a definite answer from the cell.

"Well, Mr. Barstow, you got yur answer," Homer agreed, "but there's somethin else I'd like you to think 'bout. The kids have the two basketball hoops in DoSoPa, but nothin' to really bring 'em together. Will you think 'bout organizing a couple of basketball teams that can play each other? It'll be good to keep 'em off the streets with nothin' ta do. You can coach one team an I can coach the other. I think Mr. Jake will set some hoops in cement for us so it's like a real court if we ask 'em."

"An' I cain help." Came the young voice from the cell.

Barstow wasn't expecting that kind of a request. He thought a few moments, and then said, "I'll pray about it. Incidentally, John Stoddard said he'd very much welcome my speaking in church Sunday morning. Did you give Wayne his Permission Slip?"

"Sure did, Mr. Barstow." Homer assured him.

"Good," Barstow added, "and can I just take him home from the ranch instead of bringing him back here?"

"Sure, Mr. Barstow." The deputy agreed.

As Wayne walked out of the unlocked cell and up to Barstow, the kid stopped and looked Barstow up and down.

"Yer tall." Wayne told Barstow.

The deep laugh from Barstow made the kid chuckle as the big man ruffled his hair.

.

Wayne was a really good worker. After Barstow showed him one time how to remove the screens, soap them up and hose them down, he had it, and was polishing windows like crazy.

Mia came out with some treats for the fellas, but it was hard to get the young man to stop and eat. Mia noted to Barstow that he was over-trying to be a good worker. Barstow agreed. Barstow asked Mia if she would accompany him to take Wayne home and meet his mother and brother Wilson. She readily agreed.

"Ya cain't get clean to my house," Wayne informed them, "ya have ta walk about three blocks off the road."

"That's alright Wayne," Barstow replied, "Mia and I do a lot of walking around the ranch, we like to walk."

"But….but….my home's not nice like yours," Wayne added embarrassedly, "we ain't got no money to fix anythin'."

"It's more important for a home to be filled with love than with nice things." Barstow told him.

"My mommy does love us boys, but she cries so much, and I jus' don' know what ta do." He confided with a depressed look.

Barstow gave the young man a hug, and then Mia followed suit as she asked him, "Do you guys like pizza? Thought I might order some we can pick up on the way out of town."

"Yea Maam, we ain't had pizza for a long time – i's too spensiv'." He assured her with a big grin.

When they pulled up to the Lil' Italy's Pizza, Wayne didn't wait to be asked to get out and help Barstow, he jumped out and held the door open on the building as Barstow walked in. After the pizzas, salads and sodas were paid for; the two men headed back out to Barstow's truck. Barstow needed a vehicle that would be a good work truck, and he loves red, so he bought a red Ford Club Cab, and the extra seat and doors were coming in handy right now.

Wayne rushed to open the back door on the driver's side so Barstow could set the pizzas on the seat, and then the young man put the salads and sodas in the other door and climbed in with them. The smell in the truck was overwhelmingly inviting.

Mia could see the young man's eyes through the make up mirror on her visor as she said, "Why don't you try a piece to be sure it tastes all right Wayne."

She didn't have to tell him twice, her next glance saw him inhaling the delicious vittles.

Barstow drove the truck as far up the Wood's Path that he dared, and then they loaded up the food and started walking the rest of the way. Wayne was actually bouncing along, half skipping. They could see the old trailer was badly in need of repair as they approached it.

"It even looks as if the roof leaks pretty badly." Barstow said to his wife.

There was no skirting, and the old wooden steps were all rotted, the bottom rung was broken. A couple of the windows were broken and taped together so they wouldn't fall out.

Barstow and Mia's hearts sank as she said, "What a horrible way to have to live, mostly because Mr. Close couldn't get life insurance."

Annabelle Close opened the door to welcome them. They could see two more eyes peering at them from behind her.

"That's my brother Wilson." Wayne told them as he nodded toward the eyes.

"My what a su'prise," Annabelle was saying, "didn't expect this, must a cos ya a fortune. I don ave money to pay ya."

"That's OK, Annabelle," Mia told her, "we love pizza and thought you might enjoy some too since Wayne worked so hard today. I'm Mia Perez and this is my husband Barstow. We work at the Stoddard Ranch, and have for over twenty years, ever since we came to America and became Citizens."

"Wayne got to work today?" She asked.

"He sure did," said Barstow, "and he's a mighty fine worker."

"I'm glad he did ya good, his daddie would be proud." Annabelle related.

"I understand your husband died about six or seven months ago, Annabelle," Mia was saying to her, "and it was a heart attack from Sickle Cell Disease. He was young wasn't he?"

"Yes Mam, he was only twenty-nine years old. He was a good man, an its bin eight monts now."

Annabelle started crying with grief, her husband was gone, and everyone is afraid of her, she is like an island, totally alone and so very lonely. Mia put her arms around Annabelle and held her tight.

"You're not afraid of me?" She asked Mia.

"Absolutely not," Mia assured the sobbing lady, "you're not contagious; no one can catch the disease from you. It's passed down through the parents to the kids, and that's the only way you can get it. You don't even know if you have the S-gene Trait."

Annabelle stopped crying and looked straight into Mia's eyes. She would have said more, but she was interrupted by Barstow's, "Let's eat, I'm hungry."

"Me too," Wilson's voice came from behind Barstow.

"Hi Wilson, I'm Barstow," he said as he shook the young man's hand, "your brother did a good job working today, and I think I have some more projects for him to help with. Mr. Stoddard is talking about a petting zoo on the ranch. I've been thinking, both of you boys could probably do some work around the zoo."

"A zoo? A zoo?" Wilson repeated excitedly.

"Yep, a zoo." Barstow affirmed.

"I love animals really, really, really much." Wilson added.

"So do I," Barstow said as he high-fived the kid. Now everyone was excited as they gobbled up the food.

"Now on a more serious note, Annabelle," Mia started talking, "do you know which one the genes you have? Barstow and I both have the bad S-gene trait, which is why we never had any children; we didn't want to pass the horrible disease on to our offspring. Doc Lowery would like to test all three of you to see what we can expect in the future. Will you go see him, and let the boys?"

"I don't have no money at all." Annabelle told Mia.

"It's going to be taken care of, so it won't cost you anything." Mia assured her.

"Well, I suppose. I'd like to know if my boys will suffer like their dad." Annabelle responded.

"Tell you what; Barstow is going to tell the folks in church Sunday about Sickle Cell Disease, can we pick you and the boys up so you can listen? When the people learn the truth about it, they won't be so mean to you. We've kept our traits secret until now, but Barstow is going to tell everyone we have the trait. Will you please let us pick you up?" Mia pleaded.

Annabelle paused for quite a while, thinking about the aspects of going to church, she is mad at God for taking her husband.

Mia decided to do a bit of 'bribery' as she added, "After church we would like to take you and the boys to Little Chico's Mexican Restaurant before we take you home. I love Mexican food. OK?" Mia was praying under her breath for Annabelle to accept her bribe.

When the boys heard about going out for Mexican food they started getting all excited and pleading with their mother.

"Well all right." She finally agreed.

When Barstow and Mia got home they asked to talk to John and Emily. They told them the horrible living conditions and that he was afraid he would fall through the floor at any time.

"You know Guys, Mia and I have lived almost free thanks to you guys and…."

John Stoddard cut him off with, "Yes, but God sent you two to me because I needed people I could trust, and you both are fantastic workers. So you've not received charity from us – you've earned every penny. Without your loyalty, this ranch might not have come into being."

"Thank you John," Barstow told him sincerely, "but because of your generosity we've been able to save some money, and I'm wondering what you would say to selling me a half acre of land in that clearing in the woods on Trail Road."

"What do you have in mind Barstow?" John questioned him.

"Well, I'm thinking of putting a small home spread there for Annabelle and the boys. And the boys could work at the zoo. You can take their salaries out of mine and Mia's." Barstow pleaded.

Having had many foster children, it would be nothing new to John and Emily to have a couple more running around.

"Well, no," he told Barstow, who looked a bit disappointed, "we won't sell you the land – but we'll give it to you."

Barstow grabbed John and hugged him tightly as he said,

"Thank you John, I'll still keep up with your work, I promise."

"The thought that you wouldn't didn't even cross my mind. We are family, and we take care of each other Barstow," he told the now crying man, "we'll have to get plans to the County on how we'll be putting in the septic system, and drilling a well, but that shouldn't be any problem. In fact, Todd Carson is trying to work up some plans for the Petting Zoo, and he can work on Annabelle's site plans too. I'll call him. Emily, Mia and Annabelle will have to go to the City to look for a mobile home."

Mia was smiling ear to ear; God had already answered the prayer that she had just prayed on the way back to the ranch. Sometimes God says 'yes', sometimes 'no', and sometimes 'wait', and Mia was thankful that this time He said 'YES."

John had said 'we'. He was planning on helping. God works in mysterious ways.

Confessions

As Reverend John Stoddard opened the Sunday morning service, he informed the people this was not going to be a usual service, but Elder Barstow Perez was going to speak on a subject very close to his heart. Of course the town grapevine had already announced this was happening and that's why the church was filled to capacity.

"First we will open in prayer," He told everyone, "let's all bow our heads and close our eyes."

The room hushed as the pastor opened the service with prayer for wisdom and knowledge and the blessings of Almighty God.

The first song they sang was "Bind Us Together Lord". Many in the congregation did not know the song, but the overhead on the wall gave them the words. The second song of the day would be sung after Barstow spoke.

All of the attendees were becoming silent as they read and listened to the words, "Bind us together with love."

Jake, Angela, John Stoddard, Jani and Jess had all come to hear the message. Jess had slipped into the seat next to Beth.

"Hello fellow townspeople. I so welcome you here today. We have a very special lady with us today, Annabelle Close." He pointed to Annabelle as he spoke, "Her two sons are also with us, Wayne, Jr., who is fourteen years old and Wilson who is twelve years old. This family has been through years of horror. Let me tell you about Sickle Cell Disease."

You could hear a pin drop as Barstow told the audience about how it ruins the lives of the victims, and tears families apart, through no fault of their own.

He told the packed audience how it is not a disease you can catch from anyone, you have to be born with it, it is passed down through parents, and that is the only way you can get it. Barstow told how this evil disease has robbed Annabelle of everything she ever had – including her husband Wayne Senior.

"She is bankrupt," Barstow continued, "there was no money from insurance, Wayne couldn't get life insurance. Because of the tremendous cost of drugs, they had no home; they lived with friends and in shelters. Mr. Close couldn't work; he was in too much pain. The pain of this disease is unimaginable.

Now Annabelle is a twenty-nine year old widow with two boys to raise all by herself. She has only a sixth grade education; she was never able to finish the seventh grade. But by cleaning houses and doing ironings, she somehow managed to pull enough money together to buy an old beat up trailer in the woods. When Mia and I were at her home a few days ago, I kept expecting the weak floors to cave in with me; I'm not exactly a small guy." The audience laughed as he said that.

"I was hoping it wouldn't rain because the roof leaks so badly. I was praying for no wind, because some of her windows are broken and taped together so they won't fall out and leave an open space." Barstow continued, "Annabelle couldn't get the electric turned on because having filed bankruptcy the Power Company wanted a big deposit.

Thank God they at least have water; it's run from some nice neighbors through long hoses. Her very small Welfare check isn't even large enough to give the boys lunch money for school. Can any one of you even picture having to live like this? Try for a moment to imagine her grief, what she's been through. What these two precious young men have been through. To watch their father die in so much pain. It's almost unthinkable."

The big man paused and took several big breaths before he could continue,

"Some of the worst part of the scenario is that they've been treated like they are poison by most people. They are ridiculed, harassed and made fun of. Most people shy away from them." Barstow continued, "they won't even hire Wayne to work for them for fear of being infected. Now look and listen. God loves this little family just as much as he loves each one of you. You are no better than Annabelle and her sons are, just more blessed, because you haven't had this scourge befall you."

Barstow stood silently a couple of minutes, his face grim with heartache, then he spoke as Mia come up on the podium and took his hand. "Mia and I both have the Sickle Cell S-Trait. That's why we have no children. We didn't want to pass these terrible genes on to our offspring. God has blessed us so much by putting us together with the Stoddards, and being able to watch their children grow up, and have a hand in their care. John and Emily pay us well, but just the pleasure of sharing their kids would have been compensation enough. Mia isn't barren as we've always said, but we too were afraid to let anyone know about our Sickle Cell Trait because of ignorant ramifications. Of course John and Emily have always known, but they know the truth about the disease.

Annabelle doesn't know if she carries the S hemoglobin, or if the two boys have the disease. She hasn't been able to afford to get the HPLC tests done on either one of them, but they will be tested soon. I'm not supposed to mention the Deputy's name, but he is going to pick up the tab for all three of them to get tested."

Everyone looked over at Homer since he is the only deputy in town, but Barstow didn't mention his name, as he continued, "Your pastors, John and Emily Stoddard, are giving Annabelle and the boys a lovely one-half acre piece of ground. It's on Trail Road, not too far from the entrance to the ranch, and close to us. The boys will have about two thirds distance less walk to school. The land will be developed into a spot for a new mobile home for them - without a mortgage."

John Stoddard stepped up to the Mic as he said, "But what Barstow and Mia are not telling you is that with the money they have saved for many years, they are going to buy the mobile home to put on the land. And hopefully some of you men can help clear trees and dig ditches for utilities and a stem wall. She'll also need the large deposits for her utility services."

Suddenly Wiley Ronson, the thirty-four year old blacksmith, stood up. Barstow was going to give him a Mic, but he shook his head no as he said,

"Thank you Mr. Barstow, but with my booming voice I really don't need a Mic. I want to confess that I also have the bad gene trait – which I was born with. This awful disease has robbed me of a wife and family. I didn't want to saddle a wife with the horrors that Annabelle has had to endure, nor bring children into the world just to live a hopeless life of pain. So I remained single – and all alone. In honor of the family I might have had – I want to give Annabelle and the boys Five hundred dollars. How many of you will also help this little family?"

With that Wiley walked up and handed Barstow five one hundred-dollar bills, then went back and sat down.

John Judd stood up and said he would match Wiley as he headed to the front of the church. Then Jake, then Leo, then Roscoe, then Juan Lopez from Little Chico, then Ernie Caldwell from Canyon Steak Corral, and even Sonny Boatright followed suit. Doc Lowery stood up and said he would perform the tests free of charge, so the unnamed deputy wouldn't have to come up with the money.

Ira stood up and said he didn't have the five hundred, but he would at least give one hundred from his check coming this week. Several others that couldn't afford the five hundred were now stepping up with whatever they could afford. One by one almost everyone at the meeting was giving cash, checks and promises from one dollar on up to Barstow for Annabelle and the boys. The kids were even getting involved. This was truly community action.

A hush fell over the meeting as everyone sat back down. Pastor John nodded to a young man working the overhead and asked him to put on Dan Burgess's –"PRESS ON". Pastor John also asked his wife Emily to go to the piano.

As the words appeared on the wall, everyone started singing:

"In Jesus Name we press on
Dear Lord with the prize
Clear before our eyes
We find the strength to press on"

Pastor John continued softly, "I want to thank everyone for coming today and for your participation, and I'm hoping the ladies will have a 'House Warming Party' when Annabelle and her two wonderful sons move in to their new home. Now May The Lord bless you and keep you and make his face shine down on each one of you, and may his Grace abound around you, and keep you safe and at peace – until we meet again."

Annabelle and the boys were all three crying as they stood in an exit line and each and every one of the guests greeted and hugged them. Many told them they would be praying for them. Annabelle had never felt such love.

Wiley Ronson was standing in the back of the church waiting for everyone to leave. When almost everyone was gone, he asked Annabelle and the boys if he could have the honor of taking them to Little Chico's for lunch, then take them home, he was glad he had come to church in his Chevy Bel Aire instead walking as he usually does.

Barstow didn't wait for Annabelle to answer; he resounded a happy "Yes" for them as he roughed up the hair on both of the boys.

As they were walking from his car to the Close home, Wiley was steadying Annabelle's arm so she wouldn't fall on the ruts in the road. Next time he would bring the jeep, it will go clear to the house.

Leslie Arrives

Mom and dad, along with Mia and Barstow, were waiting, as Leslie's little blue Mazda pulled in the driveway about six o'clock in the morning. The top was down and she was waving at everyone. By the time she parked Beth had joined them and all five rushed to the little car.

"Leslie Honey," Mom was saying, "it's so good to see you. It seems like forever since you were last here."

Hugs were coming from everyone, even Beth.

As Beth hugged her she identified herself, "Hi Leslie, I'm Beth, and I'm happy to meet you too."

Leslie smiled her approval as she said, "Hi Beth, I'm happy to meet you too. I understand you are doing very good here with mom and dad, and are even trying to put together a petting zoo. I think that's a wonderful idea. So Todd Carson is drawing some plans? He's always been so good at drafting doodles. I hope he is learning how to become an actual Draftsman."

"He doesn't have the money right now, Leslie," Dad informed her, "but with God's help he will be able to continue schooling for it. They don't have a computer, so he naturally doesn't know how to use one."

"Oh, OK," Leslie answered her dad, "by the way dad, who is taking the dead wood out of the Trail Road lot for you?"

But before John could answer Barstow said, "I'll go check."

When Barstow got to the Trail Road lot, he was happily surprised to see Wiley chopping and removing old stumps from the clearing.

Wiley had his old black Chevy pick up parked on the lot close to him, and it was almost full already.

"Wiley, good morning, you're up early." Barstow greeted him.

"Yea," he answered Barstow, "I saw the family's home last evening, and figured I'd better get started before too much more rain. Don't think the old trailer will last much longer. They'll have electricity and water by this afternoon in the Woods, and Harvey Lane is ordering me four windowpanes. I'm dubious about the gas cook stove, so I've got a really nice electric counter top stove I'm taking over this afternoon."

Wiley went back to work; he was on a mission.

"John has a wood pile in back of the barn for trail ride campfires. The property goes from that big rock on the back North Side to the wood's edge on the South. And from the street back to the ledge on the East." Barstow informed Wiley as he pointed.

Wiley nodded as his eyes perused the perimeter's Barstow had given him.

Barstow was smiling as he told John and Emily about Wiley working already; about the electric and water; about the stove top range; and he would be over after while to put the wood on the wood pile.

The Stoddards and Perez's went inside the ranch house to have breakfast and enjoy each other's company before they got into discussing the nasty business that had brought Leslie back to Raincroft at this time. They would have family time today, and get started on business time tomorrow.

John Judd was working at 'The Grease Pod' when an old beat up pick-up pulled in, he could see it was Lester Craddock. Lester just retired, and his wife Millie is making him clean up their spread. In the back of his old Dodge was a beat up and rusted golf cart.

"I don't want this anymore; can you find a place for it?" Lester asked John.

A few moments of thought brought John a good idea; "Sure can Lester," he told him, "just back your Dodge up to my GMC and we'll slide it right over into my truck. Here's a hundred dollars for it."

"Oh, I wasn't wanting anything for it, I just want it gone. Here's the key." Lester assured John.

"It's OK, Lester," John replied, "I think it's worth it; I have a very good use for it."

"Thanks," Lester said as he took the bill, poked it in his shirt pocket, and got into his truck and left.

John Judd covered the old golf cart well as he started for the mountain. "This will be great." He said to himself out loud.

When he got into the garage and parked he buzzed Jake to come and help him unload the old cart.

"What you gonna do with this, Dad?" Jake asked.

"Oh, I've just got an idea." Dad answered him.

Wiley dumped three truckloads of wood for campfires before he left. He went home and cleaned up, and took off for the woods in his Jeep. As he pulled up both boys came out to look over the vehicle.

Annabelle followed, "What ya need, Mr. Wiley?"

"Please just call me Wiley," he responded to her, "looks like the boys like the Jeep."

"They've never seen one before up close." Annabelle informed him.

"Ok, then let's go for a ride and get an ice cream twist at McDonald's." Wiley suggested.

The boys had already jumped in the back when Wiley mentioned McDonald's and were acting like they had just been handed a million dollars.

"Well, alright." Annabelle stammered as Wiley opened her door and helped her in the front seat.

"Seatbelts fastened?" Wiley asked. "Yes came from all three."

"Ready for take off?" Wiley quipped as he started the Jeep and backed out.

The boy's necks were zooming back and forth as they were taking in everything from a different perspective. Wiley would hook up the stove when they got back, first things first.

After they got their twists, Wiley started out Trail Road as he said, "There's something I want you to see."

As he pulled up into the beautifully treed spot, with a cleared area in the middle, he shut off the Jeep as he told the family, "This is where your new home is going to be, let's walk around it."

The boys jumped out, as Wiley went around and opened Annabelle's door, took her hand and helped her out. She was astounded as she looked around. There were wild flowers along the south side of the property.

"Will those pretty flowers be ours too?" She asked Wiley.

"Yes Mam," he answered, as he stooped over and picked four different colored tiny flowers and handed them to her.

She was talking to herself as she said, "White, yellow, pink and orange. How beautiful."

They walked around the property for a while as Wiley showed her and the boys the proposed boundaries of her new land.

Annabelle was emotionally moving in as she said, "I cain't imagin' why ya guys ar' doin' this for us. I didn' think people ar' very good anymore, but they sure ar'."

As Wiley drove into her driveway, he said, "I think we need to go to the City tomorrow and get electric blankets for your beds, I'm afraid of your old gas furnace, and I don't think it's safe - and I want you all safe."

"But ya dun' so much already, I cain't ask ya to do mor'." Annabelle responded.

"You didn't ask me, I volunteered, and since the boys are out of school for a break, they will enjoy the trip too. I'll check with Sheriff Leo and be sure Wayne will be OK going with us. I have a sign to put in the window for my customers to just leave a note through the mail slot, that I'm gone for the day. I'll pick you three up about eight o'clock in the morning. How's that sound boys?" Wiley asked the smiling faces.

The boys' noisy gleeful answer told Wiley and Annabelle they were thrilled with the idea.

Wiley walked around to get Annabelle's door, as he continued, "You'll need jackets, and a scarf for your hair."

He felt like a protector, and that was a new feeling for him.

Someone to protect and care for. He carried the hot plate into the house and sat it on top of the old stove and plugged it in as he cautioned the family, "Don't use anything but low or medium because the high setting burns a lot of electricity and will probably blow a fuse. I'm sure the wiring in this place is not safe, and I want you all safe."

Annabelle thought about how Wiley had used the term 'he wanted us safe' two times. She couldn't remember the last time someone wanted her and the kids' safe. He paused and smiled at her as he left, and high-fived both boys.

About a quarter to eight the jeep pulled into Annabelle's. The boys came running out and jumped in the jeep as Wiley got out to get his rider's door. She was smiling too. She looked lovely in the morning sunlight, and a lump came up into his throat. He could hardly keep his eyes off of her as they rode. Sometimes when their eyes met, he felt she was responding to him in a positive manner also. He felt good. She is lovely!

Emily had breakfast on the table when Leslie and Beth came down together. They had been getting acquainted up in the sitting room.

"I'm starved Mom," Leslie was saying as she sat down, "this fresh air sure increases my appetite."

"Me too." Beth added.

After they ate, Leslie asked for Ira's telephone number, and how to get to his place, it had been several years since she had been by it, and the area was a bit fuzzy.

Leslie made a stop at the sheriff's office first and introduced herself. Leo remembered her, but of course as a younger kid. Homer had heard of her, but didn't know her. She told the sheriff she had a positive identification on the DNA off the hair samples. The hairs were from a person named Otis Johnson. Leslie told him he has a huge rap sheet, with several murders, and it's been impossible to find him. He apparently heads for upper state every time the authorities are after him, and he vanishes. Her Superior had even said in joshing that they need to put out a sign 'Wanted dead or alive'.

Sheriff Leo agreed they should be wanted dead or alive, preferable dead. The two men are beasts. He was sorry there was no information on the second man, but really happy with the fact that they had named the one. Leo had heard of Otis Johnson on the National Wanted List. Leslie told him she would be going down into the Canyon with Ira and Jake.

"Does Ira and Jake know about this?" Leo asked her.

"Probably not, but they have no choice, I'm the boss." She responded.

The sheriff just raised his eyebrows as Leslie left to find Ira.

Orders & An Exchange

Ira's phone rang and he wished he could afford caller ID as he answered, he wasn't used to anyone calling him, "This is Ira."

"Ira, this is Leslie," she touted, "I need to talk to both you and Jake. Get a hold of him and meet me at the sheriff's office in about half an hour."

"OK, I'll try," Ira told her, "but I may not be able to get a hold of Jake, he's probably on a job site."

"Well find him." She ordered.

Jake's phone rang and he saw it was Ira, so he answered with a smart aleck, "Greetings and hallucinations bro, what can I do you for?"

A more somber answer came back, "Jake, Leslie's here barking orders. She wants us both in Leo's office in thirty minutes."

"OK," Jake surprised Ira with his acceptance, "we've been waiting - it's time, I'll pick you up in about twenty minutes. Sonny has to check in with the sheriff before he goes home anyway."

Jake's phone rang again; he saw that it was his lady, "Hi Jake Judd? This is Angela Crabtree."

As the big man heard her identify herself again he smirked, "Hi Baby, I love you, I should be there in about an hour and a half."

Sonny loved the way this mountain man's voice went from steel to pudding as he answered "his baby".

Someday, Sonny thought, I'll be like Jake and have a good woman – I'll be a Mountain Man too.

When Jake and Sonny pulled up to Ira's home, Sonny jumped into the rumble seat and the second big man got in the ATV.

"Guess we'll find out if she's got information on the two slimemolds." Jake remarked as they headed to the sheriff's office, he couldn't help notice Ira was freshly showered and had some stinky on, and the tips of the flowers were peeking up over his shirt pocket.

Leslie and Leo were sitting talking when the three men walked in; Sonny automatically went to his cell. Jake smiled at Leo.

"Hellooo, Leslie," Ira said to her, "you look great."

"Thanks." She responded, "Here's the info on the killers."

She didn't waste any time getting down to business. As she told the two men what was going on the extra set of ears were listening from the cell.

"We'll be going down into the canyon Wednesday morning, so do whatever you have to do to get the day clear." She added.

"You're not going down into the canyon," Ira informed her, "it's too dangerous and you're a girl."

"You don't have a choice," She informed him right back, "sure I'm a girl, but I'm also a Forensic Investigator for the State of California, so I'm the boss, like it or not! I will be going down with both of you – I need to see the area first hand. And when we find them I am the one who has to arrest them. Besides, remember, I was raised on a ranch."

As Ira looked over at Jake for support – Jake just grinned.

They talked for a while longer before they decided they would descend about five o'clock Wednesday morning. Jake told Ira he had already gotten the two new four hundred feet ropes, which they need to tie the knots in them.

"I'll help tie the knots," came an offer from the cell, obviously Sonny was taking everything in, "and I can do the ropes right now."

After Jake, Ira and Leslie left, Sonny went to the sheriff to check out as he said with a great deal of concern, "Jake's got a cast on his left arm, how is he going to be able to defend himself down in the canyon? I heard about the last episode, and it sounded really rough. I should go with him."

"Jake'll be all right, never under-estimate him." Sheriff Leo assured the young man.

Maybe I should go down with them, Sonny was thinking to himself. *I'll have to wait until I get a clear shot at the ropes and no one can stop me. I have to remember water, gloves, a rope, a jacket and a knife.* The kid had already made his decision.

Kelli was straightening a table as Todd walked into the 'Do Over'. They needed to finalize the details on the Exchange a week from Saturday.

"Good morning Todd Carson," came the greeting from Kelli, "what can I help you with?"

"Can ya take a break and we'll go check out the Dollar Menu at the Big M?" Todd asked her.

"Sure, Alice will be here, we're slow today, and I haven't had lunch yet." She answered him, knowing the reason he mentioned the Dollar Menu was because his money was tight - but that was certainly all right with her.

As they ate, Todd told her he had been in contact with both Cecil Lovett and Lloyd Ford about calling the square dance and they both agreed.

"Cecil wants to do the Progressive again," he told Kelli, "and I said all right as long as he doesn't get too fancy so the kids can't keep up."

She agreed. Kelli had talked with Mr. Bloom at the Clef, and he is excited about another Exchange. Todd assured her that he could roll Mr. Bloom's Spinet piano to the Amphitheater again; he will have his harmonica with him - and probably sing (he rolled his index finger around in a circle like a whoop de do). He said Billy is OK with playing his ukulele.

"Pam will be glad to sing; Will even offered to play his fiddle; Carrie will alternate with Mr. Bloom playing the piano; Angela will play the violin or her guitar as needed; and even Mike Crabtree said he'd bring his trumpet. Jani will bring her flute and Jess his guitar; and, of course, she [Kelli] will have her accordion." Kelli listed everything out for Todd.

"Sounds like a first class band," Todd agreed, "no one can say Raincroft is short on talent. A lot of it is from the lessons Orpha gave to the kids when they were young. By the way, how is Orpha going to get to the festivity for a spell anyway? Do I need to make plans to pick her up?"

"No, Jake is picking her up, it's pretty easy to get her in his ATV," Kelli told Todd, "and it might be hard to get her in your little Toyota.

"Are you still wanting to get some Drafting schooling?" She asked Todd.

"Sure am, in fact, I'm going on out to see John Stoddard this afternoon. He is even going to let me draft a zoo for the ranch," he responded, "are you still wanting to buy the 'Do Over' when Alice Toomey retires?"

"Sure am," Kelli responded, "been saving for a couple of years now. Don't have any idea how much she is going to want for the shop, but I'm saving anyway."

Todd pulled out some rolled up papers he had under his shirt and laid them out on the table as he said, "Here's what I've got so far."

Kelli looked over the plans with interest and made a few comments, she was obviously impressed with his work. The two sat and talked for over an hour before Kelli left to go back to work. A few single guys at the eatery were watching Todd and Kelli together, and picked up on the idea that she was probably 'off limits' now; they certainly wouldn't want to tangle with Todd – or his big brother - Ira.

Mountain Folk take care of their own, and even prowling males recognize marked territory.

Josie's cell rang; she could see it was Angela as she answered, "Hello."

"Hello this is Angela Crabtree, is this Josie Judd."

"Sure is my beautiful new daughter." Mam answered. She had waited for Angela to identify herself because she always gets a laugh out of it.

"Mam," Angela continued, "I know you don't go out much, but would you pleaz', pleaz', pleaz' go with me to pick out a weddin' gown? I don got much money, but I want ta get one my Jake likes, an' yu know what he likes bestus. I want him to be proud of me."

Mam's heart always melts with Angela's simple love for her

son, "Well, honey, Dad and I have been talking; we want to buy you your wedding gown and headpiece, along with your shoes and long underskirt."

"Yu do?" Came Angela's grateful tone.

"Yes, we sure do, and yes I will go with you to help you pick a gown out that your Jake will love. Jani wants to go too, is that OK." Mam asked already knowing the answer she would receive from this beautiful young lady.

"Oh wow," came Angela's reply, "that'd be really neat, can Kelli come too?"

"Of course, this is your party, so just say what you want," Mam assured her, "we can take Jani's little pink Volkswagen and have a blast."

"Wow, wow," was coming from Angela's end, "I get ta hav' my new mom an' sister an' my bestus frien', well, Kelli was my bestus friend, but now Jake is my bestus frien' an' Kelli is my secon' bestus friend."

Mam couldn't help but laugh at the way Angela describes things; overall her new daughter is a hoot.

After Angela finished describing everything in her words, Mam asked her when she wanted to go.

"Well we cain't go 'til after Jake comes up out of tha canyon Wednesday, so either Friday or next Monday," Angela replied, "I hav' ta be ther' 'case Jake needs me."

Mam didn't know yet that Wednesday was the day she had been dreading. It was another trip down into the dangerous canyon, and last time her son had been pretty badly injured. But she would not say anything; a mom's heart shouldn't always be spilled. Mam adored how Angela thought Jake might need her.

Mam called Jess at Nielsen's Market and asked him to bring home two boxes of energy bars and another large roll of the stretch gauze and the large size of Neosporin. Then she went down to the garage and filled her husband in on the events of the last hour.

John was working on his 'special project', the little golf cart. He had straightened the little cap like fenders, and had engine parts all over the workbench. Dad was really remodeling this little vehicle, from inside out.

Josie's husband was a bit surprised she actually committed to go out of the Mountain, but he was very glad. He hoped the wedding of his son and this little red head might promulgate her to be a bit more face to face sociable. He knew she talked to people on the outside, but many of them don't even know what she looks like. She would have to go out in public for the wedding.

Beside the paint sprayer Josie saw some turquoise metallic paint, and the larger spray nozzle. She knew what her wonderful husband was doing.

On the way to work the next morning, John Judd stopped by the sheriff's office to check about Angela being OK to ride the golf cart from her place to the mountain, and even in to the store without a license.

"She has to learn to read first," John told Leo, "and as soon as Jake and Angela are married Mam will be teaching her how to. I'll be personally responsible for any damage she does. She has to sit with her mother each day while the kids are gone to school, and it's about a five mile trip from our home to hers."

"I don't see any problem with Angela driving a golf cart around as long as you get it licensed, and instruct her on it, and it's for a short period." Leo told John.

"I'll get the cart licensed," John assured him, "and Josie will see that she learns to read enough to get her Driver's License ASAP."

The two men talked for a spell about the upcoming canyon trip, and about how much improved Sonny Boatright is.

"Wiley sure has taken an interest in Annabelle and the boys." Sheriff Leo remarked.

"That's good, Leo, it's very good." John answered.

A Good Job & Dreams Realized

"You certainly do have talent," John Stoddard said to Todd as he looked over the Plans for the Petting Zoo, "I hadn't thought about skylights so I could save on electricity, but having the panels run down each side would give light from morning to evening. I'm impressed."

"Thanks, Mr. Stoddard, now here are some septic tank proposal Plans that I think the County will OK." Todd responded.

Barstow was glued to the Plans, absorbing every detail.

As John Stoddard and Barstow perused the proposed Plans for Annabelle's laterals and water lines, they were happy to see that Todd had put the water lines uphill and the septic lines downhill. Todd had also pinpointed where the well should go because he had checked the underground geographical lay to see where the water would most likely be the most prevalent. He had also penciled in how the mobile home should lay for the best view and use of natural lighting and - solar heating.

"A fifteen degree south-southeast would give her the most heat from the sun, but I've not yet decided exactly how her home will fit into this aspect. It can probably save her quite a bit of money on her utilities. Also, there is no drainage ravine problem, so no 'Variance' will be needed." Todd was advising them.

"My goodness young man," Barstow was saying, "I'm impressed. All this and you haven't even had schooling for drafting?"

"No sir, Mr. Barstow," Todd answered, "I found out the schooling is very expensive, but I can take a correspondence course when I can afford to get a computer and learn to use it."

As John and Barstow kept digesting the Plans, John finally said to Todd, "Young man, these Plans are great just as they are. I think they are a go, what do you think Barstow?"

"Let's see what Beth thinks of them," Barstow replied, "this was her idea, and I think it would be good for her to be involved."

"Right, my friend," John told Barstow, "let's go see what Beth thinks."

The three men walked in to the ranch house as Emily was giving Beth a piano lesson.

"Can we interrupt you ladies for a few moments?" John asked.

"Sure." Emily replied.

"Beth, Todd has the mark-up Plans for the zoo, will you take a look at them and see if you want any changes." John asked the young lady.

Beth was surprised, and quite elated that someone would want her opinion on anything, especially something this important. As Todd explained the Plans to her, she took in his every word. She made a couple of comments about needing a lower sink for the little kids along with the regular height sink. Todd assured her he could make that change very easily, it just meant an extension of the pipes and a drain wye to do it, and it will take about ten minutes to redo the Plans. Then she gave her approval. It was amazing.

"Now Todd," John was saying, "you've possibly saved me several thousands of dollars for 'Plan Work'. It's obvious you spent a lot of time getting Rules and Regulations for everything. What can we do about paying you?"

"Well," Todd replied, "I've made the commitment for one hundred dollars for Annabelle, so if you could pay me the one hundred I'd be happy."

Barstow raised his eyebrows at the young man as he thought, Everyone thinks this kid is bad?

John thought a bit before he spoke, "Well no, I won't pay you one hundred dollars for all this work, Todd..."

"Well, what about fifty?" Todd cut in.

"Young man what I was going to say is that one hundred dollars is not nearly enough for all this fine work," John informed him, "I've got an idea that can help us both. We will be building more cabins and another stable, and I'll need plans for all of those. I'll get you a good computer, and pay for your Drafting Course, and you'll give me free drafting until you graduate. Does that sound fair to you?"

The young man was too emotional to speak, so he just nodded yes. Being on the 'right side' of the law really does have its rewards.

"You and I will go to the City this next week, probably Tuesday, get the Permits, and you can pick out a good computer and we'll get you signed up for Internet Service that I'll pay for until you finish your schooling. Sound OK?" John asked Todd.

Todd shook his head and then out of the blue gave the preacher a big bear hug. No one had ever given him any credit for anything. This had proved to him that he was worth something, that he could do something. He couldn't wait to tell Kelli the wonderful news. He could learn Drafting, the computer and still keep working part time at the Mark's Mill.

Todd arrived at Kelli's within minutes after Jake got to Angela's. The soon to be newlyweds were still in the greeting stage clinging to each other like they had been apart for years. When Kelli came out of her home to greet Todd, he gave her a very quick and nonchalant hug, and to his delight she gave him one back.

"Jake, come on over as soon as you can pry yourselves apart, I've got some fantastic news." Todd hollered over at the two embracing as he chuckled.

As Jake and Angela walked over to Kelli's home, Todd had already started showing Kelli the Plans, he just couldn't wait. But that was all right, he just started over again. Kelli didn't seem to mind hearing the story again at all.

"Now," Todd was summing up his speech, "I just have to figure a way to learn the computer."

"Well," Jake replied, "Mam's going to teach Ira and Angela the computer, I'll ask her if she can take one more student."

"That would be awesome." Todd responded.

This time Kelli gave him a 'congratulatory' hug without

warning. Jake winked at his soon to be wife, who winked back at her man.

After Todd left, Kelli half skipped over to Angela, "Did you see that? Todd gave me a hug." She was so happy.

Later Angela told Jake that Kelli has had a crush on Todd since junior high school, and the two of them would even sneak by his house so Kelli could just try and get a quick look at him.

"He is the only boy Kelli ever had a crush on." Angela told Jake.

"Does Todd know this?" Jake asked Angela.

"Nope." She responded.

Angela told everyone that Mam was going to take her shopping for a wedding gown, and she wanted Kelli to go with them. Kelli shrieked with delight. She told them how they were going in Jani's little car with the top down, and Mam and Dad were even going to pay for her gown. Her excitement called in the ticklebug, and soon everyone was laughing – and hugging.

It had been a wonderful day in the little town of Raincroft.

Another Canyon Trip – With a Girl

Jake hollered at Jess to tie his breakaway holster to his leg, and check to be sure the magazine was full. He picked up the two extra magazines and shoved them into his zippered jacket pocket. Since his jacket had been ripped to shreds on the last canyon trip, he borrowed his dads - telling him he would try and be careful with it.

As soon as Jess said OK on the gun magazine, Jake shoved his Colt .45 down into the holster. He slipped his two-edge switchblade knife, a bundle of stretch gauze and a pocket sized first aid kit, into a zippered pocket on his left side so he could get to them with his right hand. He had Jess put his binoculars in one of the zippered pockets on his right side; Ira could get them out for him when he needed them.

Mam was waiting to stuff the energy bars into her son's pockets as he tied the gallon of water to his waist with one of the heavy twelve feet cords. He had the second one for Ira wound around his cast. Josie also stuffed a new pair of leather gloves into his jacket.

Josie again told her son, "God go with you, my son, your dad and I love you. Remember God is still in the business of miracles. Jani and I will be in the Prayer Room covering you guys with prayer until you get back up out of the canyon."

Jake kissed his mom's cheek as he told her, "I love you too Mam."

The ATV crept down the path from the mountain and reached the turn-a-round. Jake stopped and grabbed the six-inch ball of hammock rope and the flashlight and stuffed them into the jacket. He also grabbed the small Indian blanket from off the rumble seat and stuffed it under the rope at his waistline. He hooked his set of climbing irons to his belt.

The ATV stopped at the sheriff's office to pick up the long rope that Sonny had tied all the knots in for Jake. It looked good as he threw it up on top of the bars.

When Jake picked up Ira on the way to the ranch he noted that he was loaded with gear also, including his climbing irons. Ira threw the second long rope, with all the knots in it upon the top of the roll bars too. They were both acutely aware of what they could run into. He handed Ira the second heavy twelve-foot rope, and Ira wound it around his waist and stuffed an old towel under it.

Dad and Jess would meet them at the ranch, and this time they had a little red head with them so she wouldn't be walking over ten miles 'in case her Jake needed her.' Jess was getting a bit excited about seeing Beth again.

The big man backed up the ATV to the edge of the canyon and in unison Jake and Ira each grabbed one of the long ropes, and hooked the ropes on the hooks of Jake's ATV. Dad had beaten them there and as soon as Jake shut off his ATV, dad backed right up to it and chained it to the GMC. This all seemed so familiar, and everyone sort of knew what to expect.

Leslie came out in jeans, and a plaid shirt with lots of pockets and a puffy jacket along with a heavy scarf.

"I called the media yesterday," she announced, "fed them some misinformation that will be a sure way to run the creeps into the canyon. Told them we had a lead on the killers, that they were headed north up the coastline. That should bring them this way."

"Good idea," Ira answered, "where's your gloves? You'll have blisters all over your hands, that rope leaves some pretty mean burns without gloves."

The warning barely got out of his mouth when John Stoddard came running with a pair for his daughter as he kissed her cheek.

"I know," he was telling her, "you're a big girl…But you're still my little girl."

Angela had attached herself to Jake, and he held her a few moments then nodded to his dad. As dad helped Jake unglue her, he was reminding her of how Jake could handle any situation, and besides Ira was with him again. He started guiding her to the tailgate of his GMC as he talked to her. They both hopped up on it, but as soon as Jake disappeared over the edge, she was on her feet again, and ran to the edge to watch her man descend into the vicious canyon. Ira was on the other rope; just below the top edge of the canyon wall, and Leslie was sitting on the edge ready to start down the same rope Ira was heading down on.

"Hold it," Ira shouted up to John Stoddard as he tied one end of the twelve feet rope securely around his waist.

Then threw the other end up to John Stoddard, "Tie this securely around her waist, then if she looses her grip she won't go very far, 'cause she'll have to pry me off the rope to go any farther down. And that's not going to happen."

Her dad did as he was told, even though his daughter gave him a disgruntled look.

Beth had come outside and found Jess. They were talking a mile a minute as they walked over and looked over the edge.

"Yuk." Beth said as she shivered.

Jess thought she was cold so he grabbed his jacket from the GMC and put it around her shoulders, "Here, this'll keep you warm."

She didn't tell him she was grossed out, not chilly; because his attention to her was so nice.

No one even noticed that Sonny had walked up to the edge and was watching the three descend down. He sat down close to the ropes.

When the three got down to the ledge, Ira was explaining the cave of the lady wolf where they had rescued the little girl. The rope was still dangling down from the tree in subtle memory. Sonny was taking in their every move.

Jake had Ira get the binoculars out of his pocket so they could scan the other side of the canyon. To his surprise, Leslie pulled out her pair of binoculars. Ira smiled as he and Leslie were looking for any sign of movement. They were scanning to see the rope they had seen coming down the other side on their last trip, but it wasn't visible.

"We're too far away yet." Ira remarked.

As the three repelled off the ledge, Sonny quickly slid onto the rope Jake was on, and started down before anyone could stop him. John Judd hollered at him to get back up on top, but he shouted back, "Jake might need me."

He kept on going down. Angela smiled, she was glad to have some more muscle with her man. John Judd called the sheriff to let him know Sonny had bolted over the edge to help Jake, and wouldn't be in this morning. It didn't surprise Leo one bit, and that as soon as all the 'boys' were out working, Homer was coming out to the ranch too.

With the ledge blocking the view above, the three that were already descending couldn't see that Sonny had been easily able to reach the ledge. Dad didn't want to call Jake or Ira because they would have to let go with one hand to answer the cell phone and Jake was already going one armed. There wasn't anything anyone could do right then anyway, except wait and pray.

As the young man lay on his belly peering over the ledge, he could see the vastness of the canyon. He had lived right by it for quite a while, but never had a view like this before. Every time he heard a twig blow or a rock fall, he jumped, hoping it wasn't another mountain lion.

He could see remnants of blood on the rocks, and a couple of pieces of the old bloody ropes. He shivered a bit just thinking of how dangerous of a job the two mountain men had done to rescue a little girl they didn't even know. He became emotional thinking how there really are good people in the world - even though some are pretty scary to look at. He was learning you could never judge a book by its cover that the things which are important come from the heart within. The ledge certainly was scary!

"Are you all right?" Ira asked Leslie as they landed at the bottom on solid ground.

"Yes, thank you." She replied.

"How 'bout you bro." Ira added. "Yep, I'm OK, but I think I'll sit here a spell before we go on." Jake answered.

Ira knew his bro's arm was hurting from the climb down. That climb is hard on two good arms.

"Leslie," Ira was saying, "let's walk down by the lake and look for footprints."

She nodded affirmatively as they walked the short distance to the river, and started strolling up and down the banks slowly, being careful where they were stepping.

"Let me have those gloves, you don't need to be carrying anymore weight than you have to. It'll make you tired." Ira told her as he took the gloves and stuffed them into a pocket.

"Man, you've sure changed," she told Ira, "in school you didn't care about anything or anyone."

"Well it just takes some of us longer to grow up than others." Ira replied.

It wasn't very long until Jake joined them.

"Stop, listen." Jake said authoritatively. As they all three stopped and moved their heads about for any noise. They heard a whine.

"Stay here," Jake told the two as he took off his jacket and slowly crept to the direction of the noise. It was across the river. He slid into the water, trying to hold his arm and gun up in the air to keep them dry. As he stepped up onto the riverbank, the whines were louder. Then he saw the wounded coyote that had gotten away last time, and it was circling something about ten feet from the water's edge in the brush. The coyote had lost so much blood that it was really skinny and the sore was swollen and still bleeding, obviously badly infected. It seemed like it was in lots of pain as it circled and couldn't walk very well.

It wasn't the coyote whining as Jake slowly got closer to get a glimpse of what was in distress. There she was - the lady wolf, caught in a bear trap. Jake's heart sank.

This little hero had to be rescued or the coyote would kill it. He knew he had to finish the job on the coyote, both to put it out of its misery, and because it is now extremely dangerous. Bang, a shot rang out as the coyote fell to the ground.

"Wow that was amazing." A voice said behind him. It was

Sonny; he was all wet.

Jake glanced over at Ira and Ira just shrugged his shoulders as if to say – there was nothing he could do, the kid was all ready down in the canyon.

"What are you doing here?" Jake asked him sternly.

"I thought you might need me." Sonny answered.

"I don't know whether to smack you or hug you." Jake told him.

"Well, I'd rather you hug me, I don't like your smacks." Sonny said honestly, remembering the barnyard dung.

Jake rolled his eyes and shook his head in disbelief.

"Well, since you're here, go get me a couple of energy bars out of my jacket, that's the heroic lady wolf in the bear trap and I'm going to rescue her. Also bring me the blanket laying by the jacket."

Sonny was over and back in a flash. He too knew the lady wolf deserved being rescued; she had rescued a child and was very brave – like a Mountain Wolf.

As Jake glanced back over at Ira and Leslie he saw they had problems of their own. The wolf lady's blood had signaled more creatures, and a bear was stalking them, and he figured it was the one he had rescued Muffy from. There were also a pack of three or four more coyotes. He nodded at Ira to watch his 'rear', and Ira understood what he was saying.

"Now, Sonny, since you are here, I want you to go and protect Leslie, look to the left of Ira and see what is stalking them." Jake told him.

As Sonny moved his eyes up river from Ira he could see what Jake was talking about.

"Ira's probably going to have to tangle with the creatures, and I need you to protect the lady." Jake added.

Sonny nodded as he pulled out his switchblade and headed back across the river. *I will protect a lady like a Mountain Man does, he* thought to himself.

As Sonny came up out of the river, Ira nodded his head toward the creatures, and Sonny nodded letting Ira know that he knew what was up.

"I'll stay here with the lady." Sonny whispered.

Ira had his forty-five in hand.

"How many coyotes do you see?" Leslie asked Ira.

"Five or six, but Sonny is going to stay with you." Ira told her.

Leslie hadn't seen the bear, but Ira knew Sonny had as he stepped between Leslie and the direction the creatures were congregating, with his blade out. Ira nodded at Sonny as he started slowly in the direction of the pack of coyotes. He knew sometimes a quick scare would scatter them – and sometimes not.

Jake was talking gently to the lady wolf as he sat on the ground and was very slowly inching toward her. She was still whimpering, and Jake's heart was weeping for his heroic lady wolf's pain.

"Easy little lady," he said just above a whisper, "I'm going to free you. You are such a good baby. Good girl, it going to be all right."

He was so angry that anyone would put a bear trap out to catch such a magnificent creature as this that he was fuming.

"Easy baby girl, my little hero." He kept whispering to her trying to soothe her.

He took one of the energy bars out of his shirt pocket, took the wrapper off and held it up for her to see as he kept talking softly. She eyed it. She remembered what it is. It's food, and she is hungry. Jake had no idea how long she had been there fighting off predators, she looked very weak.

He kept inching closer to the little hero; her whimpers were getting softer and softer, now he didn't see terror in her eyes from his presence. But every time she heard a noise she froze up again. He just kept sliding closer, talking softly.

Jake was finally close enough to toss the energy bar to her. It landed right under her nose. She looked at it a few seconds, up at her benefactor, then back to the bar. Pretty soon she licked the bar to taste it, and then picked it up and ate it. Jake took the wrapper off the second bar and held it up to her. She watched him intently as he tossed it to her also.

She sniffed it, then ate it, then looked back at him as if to say, "Any more?"

Now the mountain man had soothed most of her fear of him, so he inched closer to the steel jaws holding her little leg. As he was just about to open the jaws she got scared and started growling at him, so he backed off and started talking very softly to her again. He wished he had had Sonny bring him a third bar. But as he talked gently and constantly to her she mellowed again, and when the moment seemed right, he reached over and quickly shoved down hard on the trap, and as it sprang open her leg came out of it. She took off running about fifty feet, then stopped and looked back at Jake. He could see her leg was bloody, but she was putting weight on it.

"You're free now lady wolf. God please keep my little lady wolf hero safe I beg you in Jesus name." He prayed. "I'll be back to check on you little lady." He whispered after her as she sauntered off.

As soon as she was far enough away that the noise wouldn't scare her, Jake stomped the trap into pieces.

Jake was in tears when he got back across the river to Leslie and Sonny. Sonny could see his emotional condition, and it made him emotional. This Mountain Man that could pulverize any other man he'd ever seen, was as gentle as a newborn baby too when he needed to be. The young man was in absolute awe of the range and power and softness of Jake. Right then he knew he'd never been exposed to real men before, and both Jake and Ira are real men. They don't have to prove anything to anyone – except to their God.

He walked over to Jake and patted his arm as he told him, "Well done Jake."

Their attention turned up the canyon. They could still see Ira, but with no one having his back Jake headed up toward his bro. They had to take care of all eminent danger before they could get to searching for killers. Up the canyon about two hundred feet Jake could see the remnants of one of the cows John Stoddard was missing.

Leslie and Sonny followed at a safe distance, with his eyes peeling all directions watching for anything to move. Sonny had picked up the jacket and supplies that Jake had dropped, and was carrying them.

"This is kind of out of your league." Leslie snipped at Sonny.

He responded, "Shush please Miss Leslie, we don't want to make ourselves more of a target than we already are."

Sonny was right.

They hadn't walked too far behind Jake before Leslie spotted a footprint, then another one. Sonny saw them too. She took out a small digital camera and snapped photos of the prints and the general area.

Two gunshots rang out. Ira and Jake had shot up into the air to scare off the would be predators. It worked. Even the bear vanished.

"But," Jake told Sonny later, "you must never shoot a gun in the air around any kind of civilization. Here in the canyon it's all right, because there is no one to get seriously injured or killed by a falling bullet."

Sonny asked Jake if it was all right for him to check in with the sheriff and let him know all is well so far. Jake nodded yes – the kid was growing on him and Ira.

A Human Trap

The four walked on up the canyon to where Jake and Ira had found the cave of the slimemolds. They waited in the shadows for a while to be sure no one was there right then. When they started across the river, Ira scooped up Leslie to carry her across and keep her dry. She was a bit surprised, but was actually happy to stay dry.

"These slimemolds think the lady wolf is the thief of their jewelry and that's why they set the bear trap to kill her," Jake was saying, "hope they don't have too many accidents on the way up to justice."

Sonny smiled, this was the powerful Jake speaking now, and these guys were in a heap of trouble.

My, Sonny was thinking to himself, *I've been having to clean my mouth up so much lately that my mind is cleaning up too and I'm not even thinking the dirty words I've always extruded.* Jake had told him that foul words are a sign of illiteracy, and he didn't think Sonny was illiterate.

On the other side of the river all four could now see the rope hanging from the top of the canyon above them. It looked like it might be tied to a big tree on top.

"Hmmm," Jake moaned, "wonder how securely that's tied?"

"Hmmm," Ira answered him, "me to."

Jake pointed to some flat rocks that looked like they were being used for steps. Ira nodded as he took the climbing irons off the hook on his belt and put them on. Sonny had never seen such a thing as climbing irons. They looked deadly.

"Think I'll check that rope knot." Ira chuckled as he started climbing almost right straight up, stabbing his irons in at every step, using the make shift steps that the two creeps had evidently chipped out of the stickery tree stumps by brute force. The rest of the 'group' watched as Ira climbed toward the rope.

There was an alcove about twenty feet east of the cave that was perfect for listening and an occasional peek without being seen.

There was a hangman's noose on the bottom end of the rope above them.

"Reckon that's where they tie another rope so it will reach down into the canyon. Better check the knot." Ira remarked to himself as he stuck his switchblade underneath the outer layer and cut the inner cords into.

Then he moved up the rope about a foot, slipped his knife under the outer layer again and cut the inside ropes. "That won't hold much weight, and can't be seen." Ira congratulated himself as he shimmied back down the mountain wall to his waiting partners.

"Now," Ira was telling them, "they'll get part way down, then fall into the canyon, and won't be able to get back up."

"Wow." Was all Sonny could say.

Jake had known all along what Ira was going to do. "A few broken bones will be good for them," Jake remarked, "and now we wait."

Leslie didn't want to wait. She wanted to go up into the cave right then. Even though the two mountain men told her no – she had made her decision – they didn't have to be with her. She started up the wall, grabbing a hold of the bushes growing out of the rocks, amid Ira's pleas to stop and wait for the right time. A couple of the bushes she grabbed came out with her weight, she didn't think much about it. The larger bushes on the mountain were all full of stickers, and she didn't want to pick out stickers for the rest of the trip.

"Ira just wants to be king cheese," she snapped to herself right out loud.

Suddenly, bang. Here came the lady down with a crunch. Ira sprung to his feet and tried to catch her, but he was too late.

"Now look what ya done little lady," Ira was saying to her as he picked her up, "you have to wait for the right time and circumstances."

"Put me down," she demanded, "you're not so smart. I can take care of myself."

Ira could see her ankle was injured and sat her down on her feet without letting go of her weight. As she tried to stand up, it was obvious that her left ankle was injured.

"Ohhh, that smarts." She told Ira.

"You broke it." Ira informed her.

"How do you know I broke it? It's just sprained." She argued back.

"Wait a spell and it'll turn black, then we'll know." He assured her. "But we have to get that tennis shoe off you immediately while we still can."

Jake spread the blanket out as Ira approached and sat his victim down. He carefully removed her shoe. Ira then took the old towel off the rope tied around his waist, dipped it in the cool river water, and went back to the blanket. He could already see some blackness as he wrapped the cold towel around her ankle.

"Getting black already." Ira told Leslie, but she denied the fact.

"We'll just wait." Ira responded non-chalantly, as he sat down beside her and put her ankle up over his leg. She started to draw it back but he added, "We need to keep it elevated to keep the swelling as minimal as possible." She let her leg relax.

Sonny was wondering how the big man knew the ankle was broken. He knew eventually he would know 'things' too, as he grew into being a Mountain Man. Jake pulled out the energy bars Mam had sent. He gave Ira and Leslie each one.

But when he started to give Sonny one he refused saying, "You didn't pack for an extra mouth, so I'll pass."

Jake tossed it at him anyway. Jake had some of Mam's Aleve, so he gave Leslie two of them and told her to take them after she had eaten the bar. She took them without any argument, her ankle was throbbing. Everyone sat silently.

About two hours later, Leslie had fallen asleep on Ira's shoulder.

Sonny whispered to Jake, "Is Angela waiting up on top for you?"

"Yes," the big man answered, "she'll be there until I get back up."

"Man what I'd give for a good woman who will lunge at me

like she does you. But you guys are virgins and good, and I've been a rounder. There's no way I can become a virgin again." Sonny said sadly.

Jake waited a few moments studying the young man before he continued, "Sonny, God has something called his *'sea of forgetfulness'*. That means if you are really sincere and ask God for His forgiveness, and really, really mean it, that The Lord will put all your sins in His 'sea of forgetfulness', never to be remembered again. You will be totally and completely clean in God's eyes, almost like becoming a virgin again. You will be a new virgin, a God Virgin. But you can never break your covenant with God or you will come under His Almighty wrath."

Sonny was mauling over what the mountain man had told him. It was pretty heavy. Ira was also taking in Jakes words and his mental wheels were also turning.

A noise came from the area of the rope of misfortune. Then a voice shouting to someone else that hopefully they'd gotten that blankity blank wolf that had been stealing their stuff.

Jake knew for sure his lady wolf's misery was because of these two slimemolds.

Ira gently bumped Leslie to wake her up. Ira pointed to the rope as she opened her eyes. Leslie pulled out a tape recorder, turned it on and held it up in the air as she put her index finger across her lips indicating silence. She had her camera lying beside her. Sonny picked up the camera and slipped over to the edge of the alcove, held it up to his eye and waited quietly. Leslie nodded at Ira; the kid was doing all right.

A scream filled the air as the first man came tumbling down the canyon wall. Sonny had stepped out and gotten a picture of him as the second one came tumbling down. Snap – his fall was on camera too.

Jake had stood up by then and joined Sonny as he said, "Otis Johnson I presume."

"What the H___? Who are you?" the man said as he screamed in pain.

The other man laying about ten feet from his partner was

screaming also. Ira had picked up Leslie and was holding her as she showed the two scoundrels her badge and announced,

"I am Leslie Stoddard, Special Forensic Investigator for the State of California. You both are under arrest for Rape, Murder and Grand Theft. You have the right to remain silent, anything you say can and will be used against you in a court of law. You have the right to have an attorney present during questioning. If you cannot afford an attorney, one will be appointed for you. Do you understand these rights?"

She was still recording.

"Good job." Ira whispered in her ear.

Sonny had gotten lots of pictures.

Leslie recognized the one man as Otis Johnson. She asked the other man his name, but he wouldn't answer.

"Suit yourself," she told them as she spoke to Jake and Sonny, "now gentlemen if you will kindly secure these gentlemen so they can't run away, I'd be most grateful."

Jake knew they had broken bones; it was pretty obvious with their screams and distortions. He smiled as he took a big roll of duct tape out of his jacket.

He glanced at Sonny as he said, "Wanna help."

The young man grabbed the roll of tape, tore off a big piece of it, and began taping one of the men's mouth's shut as he wound the tape clear around his head.

"I don't want to listen to all that racket." Sonny told Jake.

Jake tore off a strip and ran it around Otis Johnson's mouth and head; "I don't want to listen to all that racket either."

Now there were only muffled screams.

"Dang," Leslie spoke up, "you guys are two peas in a pod."

Man was that an accolade to Sonny.

"I'd put you down, but looks like I'm not needed to hog-tie these two creeps." Ira said to his bundle of feminine flesh.

"Just don't kill them." Leslie told the guys. She had turned off her recorder – to save the tape.

"Here's a piece for Missy." He told Otis as he ran a long piece of the duct tape around the creep's arms three or four times amid his screams.

"Here's a piece for Missy." Sonny told the creep he was working on with the same rounds of duct tape, amid his muffled screams.

"Here's a piece for Missy's dead mother and father." Jake told Otis as he yanked out his crooked leg and duct taped it to the other one from the ankle to the knee, as the creep bolted in pain.

"Here's a piece for Missy's dead mother and father." Sonny told the creep as he yanked one of his legs straight and duct taped it to the other one from the ankle to the knee. The second creep was also bolting in pain.

"Now we'll tape their legs together so we can drag them with us." Jake told Sonny as he was dragging the creep over by Otis. The two started taping their legs together.

"OK, Leslie, now we can check the cave. Give me your camera and we'll get some pictures for you." Jake was saying.

"Umm," Ira answered, I think I'd better go up to the cave, you need your good arm in tact to drag these scumbags."

Jake nodded, and Leslie gave him the camera after he sat her back down on the blanket.

Ira put on his gloves; he still had his climbing irons on, and started grabbing large stumps and weeds poking out the side of the canyon. He stabbed his irons in each step of the way. When he got up to the ledge in front of the cave, he took several pictures. The steel box had been moved, and was locked again.

"Look out below." Ira hollered and everyone stepped back.

Crash, the box hit the ground.

Ira tossed the camera to Sonny, "Here, take some pictures of me up here at the cave for posterity. Sonny caught the camera, and started taking lots of pictures of everyone and everything.

As Ira shimmied down the side, he 'accidentally' lost his footing and landed on the two men lying beneath the cave. His spikes had penetrated the duct tape on both of them.

"Oops, sorry." He snorted at them. He hadn't had the fun of taping them up, and he wanted to get in on the action.

Now the problem was how to get them across the river without drowning them. This would take all three men. After Jake and Ira laid their guns on the blanket beside Leslie, they walked over to the two men. Jake picked up the duct tape between the feet, and the legs of both men came up off the ground. Ira and Sonny each picked up the shoulders of a creep, and the men were airborne amid their muffled shrieks of agony.

"I'd prefer to let them drown, but I can't honestly do that, God wouldn't like me to kill them like I want to." Jake was saying as they entered the water with the men held in the air.

Once on the other side, they dropped the two to the ground. Otis was still screaming, but his partner had evidently blacked out with pain. Ira went back for Leslie, the guns and camping supplies, and Sonny for the steel box.

"Sonny," Ira said to him, "I was upset when you came down into the canyon, but I must say we couldn't have completed this job this fast without you. Thanks."

"Thanks." Sonny replied, he felt like a mountain man now.

Jake drug the men to the climbing ropes by the duct tape holding their legs together. Their backs and heads were banging on the rocks; weeds and hills as they moved over the terrain; kind of like the old western movies where the horses would drag people.

Ira had helped Jake put his jacket back on. It was pretty obvious that Jake was in a lot of pain. Sonny kept watching the strength, power and determination of this big man.

He shook his head once as he kept mumbling to himself, "Jake can battle bears – and he's still a virgin. Wow, he's about as far from a sissy as anyone you'll ever meet anywhere, and he's still a virgin. It takes a real man to remain 'in tact' for his marriage. A wimp can't control himself. Jake said I could be a God Virgin." Sonny was remembering everything Jake had told him.

Ira wet the towel in the cold water again and re-wrapped Leslie's ankle. Then he carried a grateful Leslie with her rapidly swelling black ankle across the river and headed to the ropes. She noted the white card sticking up out of his pocket and pulled it up to see the pretty flowers. She smiled at him and put the little card back in his pocket.

Sonny carried the heavy steel trunk; he was using his brawn for good this time.

When they reached the bottom of the climbing ropes Jake said they would tie the prisoners up with one of the twelve foot heavy ropes like Indian Papooses, and hook the big rope that Ira was going up first to the captives.

Ira told to Sonny to take the second twelve-foot rope and tie it around Leslie's waist, and then around his [Ira's]. After they got to the top, Ira would pull the two scabs up to the top with the ATV. Ira said they'd wait until everyone was out of the canyon before calling the Paramedics, they didn't want to rush anything. He wanted to bring them up feet first but Leslie had asked them not to kill the creeps.

Ira and Leslie stood there a few moments.

"Great, how do I get back up?" She asked Ira, "It looks like I'm just going to dangle in the air below you."

Instead of answering her Ira set Leslie part way down, then put his shoulder into her waist and slung her over it. She kicked a few times trying to say no, but he had started up the rope. Jake started laughing at the sight, and Sonny joined him.

Jake called his dad and told him Ira and Leslie were on their way up and that she has a bad ankle. Dad said he'd call Mam and let her know that things are OK.

Jess and Beth were still talking a mile a minute as they sat on the edge of the canyon watching down for any movement.

Jake paused a moment, then he walked back over to the water's edge. To his delight he could see two beautiful eyes watching him from the weeds, and they were moving. His lady wolf would be all right. He took the wrappers off of two more energy bars and lay them about ten feet from the water's edge. He couldn't see her injured leg, but she was moving.

Sonny watched the gentle big man with his friend; one moment a decisive and aggressive powerhouse, and the next moment a gentle and caring protector. Sonny tied the steel box to the end of the second hanging rope, to be pulled up as soon as Jake and he were safely out of the canyon. Sonny watched Jake's every move. Power and gentleness – who'd a thought, the young man was thinking.

Sonny asked Jake to go up first. Jake didn't want to, but Sonny told him – we can either do this little job peacefully – or not. Jake snickered. Sonny told him he could wait down there all evening if Jake wouldn't go up first with his injured arm.

Boing, a light went on in Jake's head. If Ira's going to pull the creeps up, he can just pull us up at the same time, since there wouldn't be anyone else behind needing the long ropes. With the ATV hooked to the GMC, the two of them together would have enough power to pull the two creeps, the steel box and the two men up at the same time – as long as one of the ropes didn't break.

"We'll just have to pray." Jake told Sonny as he called his dad back to tell him the idea. Jake would take the rope with the creeps, and Sonny would take the other rope with the steel box.

As Ira and Leslie got to the top, Dad and John Stoddard were waiting to pull them over the edge onto level ground.

"That's quite a way to scale a mountain," John Stoddard joked at his daughter, really happy that she was OK. She gave him a 'pouty' look, but didn't say anything.

"Careful of her left ankle, it's broken and shouldn't have any weight put on it," Ira ordered, "she slipped and fell."

As Leslie took off the towel to show her dad the ankle, it had turned black. She looked over at Ira and grinned.

Dad told Ira what Jake had said to do, so Dad started the GMC and Ira started the ATV. "I'll hold my arm straight out the window, and when I drop it, we'll both hit the gas slowly at the same time."

Dad buzzed Jake, "Are you guys ready?"

"Yep." Jake replied; he and Sonny had taken their respective places on the ropes.

"Now we go up together," Sonny chuckled.

Dad stretched his arm out of the GMC window, waited a few seconds to be sure Ira was ready, and then dropped his hand. Both vehicles started moving forward slowly. A jerk told them the ropes were tight. The knots on the ropes could be felt as each one moved above the canyon edge and onto the ground. Bump, bump, bump. Angela was watching each and every knot come up onto the surface; she knew her man was coming back to her.

As Jake's head appeared at the top of the wall Angela was on her belly, already kissing it, and helping to pull him up as the knots continued popping up over the top edge. John Stoddard was trying to pull him up on the ground too amid her tears and kisses.

Jake knew he'd better give her something to do, so he told her to call Mam right away and tell her what's going on and that they're all safe. Man was he glad he had gotten her a cell phone.

Sonny's head appeared over the edge, and Homer and Jess were there grabbing him to help him get up on the solid ground.

"You're a hero too Sonny." Homer's words rushed deep into Sonny's heart, and they felt so good.

As soon as the two mountain men were on the top they watched down the wall as the creeps and the steel box came up to the top.

Sheriff Leo was grabbing for the men as Jake told him, "Funny thing, Sheriff, the rope they were climbing on broke and they fell down the mountain and hurt themselves. Sonny got some pictures of both of their accidents."

"Funny thing," Leo smiled, "we'll see what Leslie wants done with them now. Have they been read their Miranda Rights?"

"Yes, Leslie identified herself immediately and read them their rights. It's all on tape." Jake told the sheriff.

After Sonny and Jess pulled the box on up onto the level ground, Sonny slid it over to Leslie sitting on the blanket Ira had put back down for her.

"Sonny," she said to him, "you weren't out of your league. I'm sorry I said that. You did a wonderful job. Thank you."

"You're welcome, Miss Leslie." Sonny answered.

Leslie asked for a hammer, and a cameraman. Sonny nodded as he took the camera and started taking more pictures. Ira grabbed the hammer and whacked the lock and it fell off. Leslie opened the trunk, and sure enough, there was more stash in it. There were obviously more victims.

"The State Forensic Laboratory will be very interested in the trunk," she was telling the sheriff, "I just have to figure a way to get it back to the office. Doesn't look like I'll be driving for a week or so."

It's gonna be longer than that," Ira chimed in, "we'll just put the box in your trunk, lock it and I'll drive you in your car. Jake can follow me on the bike to bring me back."

"Sounds like a plan." Agreed Leslie.

Homer, Jess and Sonny threw the killers in the back of the sheriff's Hummer.

"They'll have to go to City Hospital, and I can make it there faster than the paramedics, I'm already here." The Sheriff was saying.

"I'll call my office and get a couple of strong arms to come from LA and stay with them until they can be moved. Then take them back to LA for justice. The sheriff in the City can take custody of them from us until the big boys get there to pick them up," Leslie told the sheriff, "I'll need to go with them for the transfer and to check them in."

Leo said great, that they could both go in his Hummer and he would bring her back as soon as the transfer had been made.

Ira told the sheriff he would be going too, Leslie couldn't put any weight on her ankle, and he'd have to carry her. Ira reminded the two that she had to get medical attention too, that getting her fixed was much more important than getting the slimemolds fixed. Neither argued with him.

Angela was now in her beloved's arms and he in hers, and the two didn't care who was around them as they held each other close.

"I'll take Sonny home, Mr. Jake." Homer was saying to the big man, but he wasn't listening.

As Sonny watched, he knew some day, he would have his own Angela – or Pam. And it too would be right and proper. Jess gave a quick good bye squeeze to Beth, and then climbed in Dad's Jimmy. Dad told Jess it looks to him like Jess may have more than a passing interest in Beth, but Jess only smiled.

When Homer pulled into the Rainrest Motel, there were only two cars there.

"Not much business this week, so hopefully Marcus was able to handle everything." Sonny was saying.

Marcus Bates is the 'Motel Manager' that comes around once a month to pretend he is running the motel – so the Boatrights won't get in trouble for having an underage kid running the place.

After her x-rays at City Hospital, the break was confirmed and the doctor's had to cast Leslie's ankle. Ira had been asked to leave the room while they worked on her, but he sat down right beside her while the doctors were casting her ankle. Neither of the doctors seemed to want to challenge the scruffy big man.

Leslie could tell Ira was having a hard time refraining from giving orders to the doctors; his eyes were totally fixed on exactly what they were doing to her. It was almost midnight when they finished. They wanted to keep her overnight but she refused. The doctor ordered her some antibiotics.

"We'll need some crutches for her too, and make them the aluminum ones so they're not too heavy for her." Ira ordered.

The doctors told her to stay off her foot for at least forty-eight hours before putting any weight on it at all. After that she could use the crutches, as long as she just slid her ankle and didn't put much weight on it. The nurse said she'd go get Leslie a chair to wheel her out to the sheriff's Hummer, but Ira told her not to bother as he gently picked Leslie up and was holding her so her ankle didn't touch anything.

The nurses had a terrible time getting all the duct tape off of the creeps, but when they heard what they had done, there wasn't any sympathy for them in the hospital. Three men from the sheriff's office in the City had met them in the emergency room, and the transfer of custody had taken place.

Sheriff Leo told the City Sheriff about the trail of blood the two had left, how slippery they were, and they would need watching 24-7. An officer would be with each of them at all times to be sure they didn't escape again - the City Sheriff assured Leo. But, with all their broken bones, it wasn't likely they would get very far.

Leslie called her boss, and told him the story. He decided she would take a mandatory couple of weeks off, and her folk's ranch would be a good place to recuperate where she would have help and comfort. He would send an extra Agent to the hospital, and he could go to the ranch and pick up the steel box and bring it back along with fresh DNA samples of the killers.

He also wanted the audio tape proving they had been read their Rights, along with the camera card proving they fell on their own. The State had an airtight case thanks to the four brave people. He also mentioned to her that the Newspaper had gotten an anonymous tip about the whereabouts of the murders, and the cops closing in on them – which proved to be wrong.

Leslie didn't answer.

A Mercy Trip

Doc Lowery had barely got his office door open the next morning when Jake showed up.

"Morning Jake." The doc greeted cheerfully. "I understand you had another successful trip down into the canyon."

"Right." Jake answered, "But I have to make another trip right away. How much anesthesia will it take to give a beautiful lady, approximately eighty pounds, a couple hours sleep?"

"You mean the beautiful lady wolf, right?" Doc asked.

"Yes." Jake affirmed. "I also need a long acting shot of antibiotics, and some antibiotic cream that is waterproof and won't hurt her if she ingests it. Will you fix me up?"

"Sure." Ed responded as he moved to unlock his pharmacy cabinet.

As Jake got into his ATV, he pondered that Ira was pretty busy right now, and probably extremely tired after being up all night, so he'd just go pick up the irons. He would then find Deputy Homer.

"Guess I'll see what the young Deputy is made of." Jake said right out loud as he drove to Ira's.

As soon as he retrieved the irons from Billy, he headed for Nelson's market. He bought a pound of fresh ground hamburger. He could put the anesthesia in the hamburger.

Deputy Homer was in the office as Jake walked in, working on the computer. Homer was always doing research on the computer – and studying English.

"Good Morning Mr. Jake." Homer said cheerfully as the big man sat down at his desk. "What can I do for you?"

Jake noticed Homer's voice was calm; he was so engrossed in his work he didn't think about being nervous.

"I want to borrow you for a dangerous trip, Homer." Jake remarked to him, waiting for a rejection or excuse.

But none came. Instead Homer stood up and asked, "Will I need my gun?"

Jake snickered. "Possibly."

"Where are we going?" The young Deputy asked.

"To treat a lady wolf." Jake responded.

"Figgered you would, Mr. Jake." Homer said calmly.

"You're not afraid to go down into the canyon, Homer?" Jake questioned.

"Nope." Homer responded as he left Leo a note he would be gone for several hours, maybe all day.

The two men jumped in the ATV and headed for the ranch. Jake didn't want to bother anyone for this short trip, and would just tie the ATV to a couple of big trees close to the edge of the canyon.

Homer had already tied the climbing irons on his belt as they got out of the ATV, and each took a thick rope and tied it to one of the front hooks on the ATV and secured it around a couple of large trees.

As Jake went to pick up the big climbing rope with the knots, Homer had already secured it to one of the big hooks on the back of the vehicle.

John Stoddard walked up to them as he said, "Good morning gentlemen. Can I help you with anything?"

"Good morning to you, John." Jake greeted as he looked for the sack from Doc Lowery.

The sack, extra rope and jug of water were missing. As Jake turned around to see what Homer was doing – Homer was no where in sight. Jake and John both walked over to the edge of the canyon and looked down. There on the ledge was the young deputy, loaded with the supplies and waiting for Jake to catch up with him.

The two men glanced at each other, and back down into the canyon.

"Homer's fast." John remarked.

"He sure is." Jake replied as he backed down over the edge grabbing the rope with his right arm.

"I'll hook my pick up to your ATV." John added.

Homer was wide eyed as they hit the bottom of the canyon. He was listening to the various sounds. Jake knew being born and raised with the wild animals, Homer was keenly aware of animal noises.

"Where do you usually see the lady wolf?" Homer whispered.

"Up there about fifty feet and not too far from the water's edge." Jake whispered back.

Homer crept quietly up the river about thirty feet and sat down silently. Jake was really intrigued as he watched the young deputy. Then Jake crept up and sat down beside him.

About fifteen minutes later Homer pointed to a patch of brush. Jake smiled at the young man for having heard what he had. There were the two eyes watching them. Jake's heart leapt up into his throat. His little heroine was still alive.

"Thank you Heavenly Father." Jake prayed gratefully.

Homer watched the wolf a few moments than started talking softly to her, "Hi little lady, we're here to help you. Come on over, we have a treat for you."

Jake watched in amazement when the little lady came over and lay down about ten feet from where they were sitting as Homer kept talking just above a whisper to her. She didn't seem to have any fear of Homer. Jake would have scratched his head, but thought his sudden movement would scare her. Her leg had dried blood all over it, and looked swollen.

Homer slowly and gracefully unwrapped the meat and took about a fourth of it and slowly handed it to Jake, his voice never hesitating as he talked to the young lady. Jake quietly put the anesthesia powder into the meat, and then handed the ball back to Homer. Jake was so in awe and engrossed with how Homer was reaching out to this wild animal, and it was responding back to him, he was letting the deputy take the lead.

Jake had always had a reciprocal relationship with animals, but it seemed like this young man actually talked the lady's language.

The little heroine seemed to know what the deputy was saying to her. Jake had never witnessed an animal responding to a human being like that – not even to himself.

The lady watched as Homer slowly gave the ball a nudge and it rolled down the bank to her. She sniffed it a couple of times – then gulped it down. Neither man moved. They would just wait as the little lady lay back down as if on cue.

About twenty minutes later, she laid her head down and shut her eyes. She had gone to sleep.

Homer stood up and slowly and quietly walked up to her. He began to stroke her fur. She didn't move so he motioned Jake to come on over.

Jake started examining her leg. He couldn't feel any broken bones, but the leg was swollen. He took out the hypodermic and gave her the antibiotic injection in her leg muscle just above the wound.

Homer had found an empty water jug, and went to the creek and filled it with fresh water, and was cleaning the blood and gunk off the wound. Jake examined it more, but still didn't find any bone damage.

As Homer held up the salve, Jake rubbed it off onto his finger and gently worked it deep into the cleaned wound. He rubbed the salve down under the fur into the meat surrounding the injured area. He knew she would be licking the salve off, but hopefully it would be on the wound long enough to penetrate deep enough she couldn't get it all off.

Jake's heart was joyous as the two men stood up, a job well done. They nodded at each other as they walked back to the spot they had been sitting.

Homer took the rest of the meat, and formed it into small balls, then took it over and laid them down on the ground, some about two feet from her snout, and more about four feet away. She would have to get up to reach the meat, which would allow the men to be sure she could walk.

The men started talking softly about small things.

"So where are your parents now? I know they've been gone for several months." Jake asked him.

"My Grandma Newman is dyin from cancer, an – an - and they will stay with her as long as necessary." Homer replied.

Jake couldn't help but notice that Homer was speaking rather slowly and trying to annunciate words better. "How far did you get in school? As I recall it was to the ninth grade." Jake asked the young deputy.

"I didn' finish the ninth grade, dad lost his job an' we didn have the money. I had to work an - and bring some in." Homer responded.

"You seem to like your job." Jake remarked.

"I do, Mr. Jake, I really like law enforcement." Homer agreed.

Jake noticed three coyotes up the river from them and hoped he wouldn't have to tangle with them again. Homer was watching them too, and turned his body slightly diagonally to face them eyeball to eyeball. They were obviously smelling the fresh hamburger.

"What are you studying on the computer? You're on it every time I go by."

 Jake inquired.

"I'm studyin - studying English – an' law enforcement. I need to lern to talk better so I cain get a good payin' job to support a wife – er – a – er – one that is of age." Homer stammered.

Jake chuckled to himself – knowing his little sister was the 'one that is of age' the young man was referring to.

"This lady - who is of age – do you think she is interested in you?" Jake investigated.

"Well sir," Homer stammered, "I have watched her watching me…I mean if there was a young lady – of age of course – I might watch to see if she was watchin' me – an if she was, if there was a lady – I'd probably someday get up nerve to ask her – if she was of age – an it'd be OK to ask her – if there was a lady…"

"I get the drift, Homer," Jake cut in because it didn't look like the young deputy knew how to finish the sentence.

Homer was also trying to get the point across to Jake that he knew under aged ladies are jailbait. Jani's only seventeen.

About an hour later the lady wolf moving interrupted their conversation. She was waking up. Now they could see her condition. Neither man moved.

Homer started whispering to her, and she eyed him for a moment, and then tried to stand up. It took her a few tries, but finally she was up on her wobbly legs. She sniffed towards the first meatball, took a couple of unsteady steps. She sat back down as she picked it up. Then on her feet again she went for the second meatball. By the time she was headed for the third meatball she was getting her equilibrium. She was putting more weight on her leg as she became stable.

The men smiled at each other. They would wait another hour before they headed back up the rope to be sure none of the coyote's came her way.

Homer stopped in mid speech. He looked down river. The brush was cracking as the sound moved closer. Homer grinned at Jake as two eyes showed through the bushes. Jake knew wolf eyes, as did Homer.

A form finally came into view; it was a large male wolf. Jake poked Homer with his elbow. The little lady had found a mate, and he was a big dude. They knew it was her new mate, because he wouldn't ordinarily come so close to a human. But he was there to protect her.

He saw the two remaining meatballs on the ground, but made no move to steal them from her. The big male knew she needed the nourishment, as he got close enough to her to sniff her wounds. He looked up at the two men as if to say "Thank you" and the men were so moved they both had tears in their eyes. She now had a big mountain fella to care for her.

About thirty minutes later, the lady wolf and her mountain wolf sauntered off down the river and out of sight.

The two men waited in silence for about ten minutes, each knowing the other was pondering what had just happened in their heart.

Homer insisted that Jake go up the rope first because of him having only one arm. Jake looked at the steadfastness of Homer's countenance, and decided to cooperate. When he got to the ledge, he turned and looked down, and the young deputy was bolting up the rope.

Jake headed on up to the top edge, and to his surprise he had an audience. Jake's dad and Angela were both waiting for them. Plus, Jani had come with Dad…just to see what was going on…

Homer was up the rope and on the ledge so fast no one had a chance to help him. He saw Jani watching him from the top, and she was smiling at him.

"Yes Sir," John Stoddard said to Jake again, "Homer is fast."

An Exchange & Claiming a Family

Todd pulled into Kelli's driveway about six A.M. on the 21st. He would be taking Kelli, Pam and Will in his little Toyota. He had completely cleaned out the trunk of his car to hold Kelli's accordion, Will's fiddle and three blankets. He had even washed the little vehicle. Will had his harmonica in his shirt pocket, and his usual 'sit backness' was replaced with excitement.

As Todd walked up to the door and Kelli stepped out he gave her a quick 'hello hug', which she returned. She noticed Todd had trimmed and combed his beard; his nails were neat; and he had stinky on. The festivities didn't start until eight o'clock, but he didn't want to be late, and they could make set-up plans.

Nelli would be staying home; her husband was to be there sometime that afternoon. Walter would be home until Monday, then off on the road again. Perhaps they would hop over later.

When the little Toyota pulled up to the amphitheater Wiley Ronson was already there sitting on one of the concrete steps, deep in thought.

"Good morning Mr. Ronson, it's gonna be beautiful out today." Todd said cheerfully to him.

"Beautiful? Yea, she sure is." Wiley mused back – but came back to reality and realized Todd was talking about the weather, "Yep, it's going to be a good day."

Todd grinned at Kelli as he changed the subject to cover Wiley's embarrassment; "Will you help me roll the piano over from The Clef?"

"Absolutely." Wiley responded with a sign of relief, halfway believing they hadn't heard his little blunder. It was rare for Wiley to get excited about anything – he had become resolved to having a lonely and unexciting life – and no family. But every time he lays his eyes on this Annabelle lady, his heart starts going pitter pat, pitter pat. It is a joyful feeling, and he really likes it. And those two boys, they're some of the best looking kids he's ever seen.

But, he reminded himself, Annabelle's only been widowed for seven or eight months, and hasn't been through the grieving cycles yet, so he must keep everything platonic for now to not scare her off. Besides, he doesn't want to make the boys become defensive toward him; he knows he can never replace their father, but he would be honored to be their stepfather and take care of them.

The powerful man knows he must really give the situation to God; ask his blessing, wisdom and guidance. He could hardly wait for eight o'clock to roll around so he could pick them up. Moving the piano slipped his mind as he decided to go out and talk to Barstow while waiting for time to pass.

Barstow was checking the cattle as he pulled in.

"Good Morning," the booming voice shouted to Barstow, "I want to talk to you. It's pretty important."

Barstow stopped what he was doing and walked over to Wiley and the booming voice continued, "I'm going to buy the home for Annabelle and the boys, you save your money."

"Ummm, what?" Barstow asked.

"I said I'm going to buy the home for Annabelle and the boys, so you keep your money. And, the money raised for her at church can go into Trust Funds for the boy's educations." Wiley reiterated.

Barstow's head was shaking as he was trying to take in what Wiley was saying.

"I've been thinking about this quite a bit, and I've made a decision, I'm going to marry Annabelle and her boys." Wiley continued.

"Ummm," Barstow replied, "does Annabelle know this?"

"Not yet, she's not had her grieving time. I'll wait a while before I tell her, but I know she'll like the idea," Wiley responded, "now don't say anything to anyone; I want it to be a surprise."

"It'll be a surprise all right Wiley," Barstow agreed, as he started chuckling.

"Next week I'll take her and the boys to the City to pick out a home they will all like. The boys should have their say in the choice too. She doesn't need to know anything except that she's got the money to buy what she wants," Wiley continued, "she deserves the best, so do the boys. No one's going to push them around again, nor will they ever want for anything. She is a beautiful and terrific woman, who has held it together through all the tremendous horrors that have besieged her. I'm not going to let a catch like that get away. I've been praying, and God knows I want my own family, and I believe he's giving them to me."

"Man, Wiley," Barstow was still searching for words, "I've always known you are a man who can make a decision, but any possibility you have the cart before the horse?"

"Nope," Wiley stated flatly, "I knew the Lord would answer my prayer because I've been faithful. That's my family, and even if the boys end up having Sickle Cell, we'll deal with it together, they won't be alone. I've been having a pretty stern talk with God about that situation too."

Barstow Perez was flabber-ghasted, and really at a loss for words when John Stoddard came up and noticed him fumbling to get some out.

He also noticed Wiley with a very determined look so he asked, "What's up? You two look pretty serious."

"I am, I've made some decisions." Wiley told John Stoddard as he relayed the facts to him.

Wiley finished up with, "Gotta go pick up Annabelle and the kids for the Exchange. Probably see you both there. I need a bill for what you've paid out so far. You guys know I've had my shop since I was a teenager, I received my dad's large life insurance, and have had nothing to spend my money on. Now I do."

As the booming voice drove away in his jeep, Barstow and John started laughing, it was serious, but it was funny. Sometimes Wiley can be a bit unorthodox, however underneath all that gruffness is a wonderful and honest Christian man.

Most of the musicians had arrived at the amphitheater, and were tuning up their instruments. People began laying out blankets and tables with their wares. Folding chairs started to line the sidewalks, chatter was high. Kids were excitedly running everywhere to see what other kids had shown up. Shoppers could be seen picking up things they needed. It seems as though no one takes things they don't need, just to be taking them. It's the honor system in full swing.

Todd and Will had already brought over Mr. Bloom's piano, and Kelli was playing it. Todd's beautiful deep baritone voice was half singing with her as he arranged things. Kelli started singing with him and soon he joined her on the bench so they could duet. He kept smiling at her, and she was smiling back.

A bit later, here comes Sonny up to the piano.

"Mr. Carson," he was saying to Todd, "I want your permission to dance with Pam. I promise and swear I will behave myself, and be absolutely proper. I will treat her like the lady she is, and we'll not leave your sight."

Kelli grinned as Todd was thinking. Ira had told him what a really good thing Sonny had done in the canyon and around the town lately. How his attitude has totally changed about life, and how very badly he wants to be a real man.

Finally after keeping the kid in suspense for a few moments, he said, "OK, but you can't take her out of my sight."

"I won't, I promise. Thanks Mr. Carson. Now, please excuse me, I've got to go see Deputy Homer, I will be helping him today." Sonny answered gratefully.

Jess had called John Stoddard to see if it was all right to ask Beth to ride to the Exchange with him, and John Stoddard had agreed. So as he pulled into the ranch he felt happy. He walked up to the door and knocked. Beth answered.

"You look beautiful as usual." Jess told her as she initiated a hello squeeze.

"Let's look at the place for the Petting Zoo first." She suggested.

Things had been so much in an upheaval the last time he was there at the ranch that they hadn't had time to really look at the area. He was certainly all right with looking at it now; it would give them one more thing they could talk about.

As Beth showed him around, he asked her if they were putting together a 'Non-Responsibility Affidavit' for visitors to protect the ranch. She didn't know, but would certainly mention it to John and Emily. He stepped inside the ranch house with her as she went to grab the new purse Emily had bought her. John was reading in the den.

"Jess has some paper he wants to ask you about." Beth told John Stoddard.

"What kind of a paper, Jess?" John asked.

"Well Sir, it's called a 'Non-Responsibility Affidavit' for visitors to sign so your ranch won't get sued if someone gets hurt on it. It's different than your existing Affidavit, because it should cover the children with the animals." Jess informed him.

John let it roll around a bit in his thoughts before he spoke again, "Well Jess, sounds like you have a good point, perhaps you can draw something up for a sample of exactly what you are talking about?" John inquired.

"Absolutely. I'll have it for you within a couple of days." Jess assured him.

Both Jess and Beth were grinning at each other as he shut his Mazda's door behind her. The top was down, it was beautiful outside, and he had a gorgeous blonde with him by permission. Life is good.

As Wiley's camouflage Jeep pulled into his family's driveway, the boys came running out and hopped in. The booming voice went to the door to help Annabelle down the steps and into the jeep.

"Good morning everyone." He said jovially as he looked right into her eyes.

"Good Mornin'." Rang out from the back seat - and the front seat.

Yesss, Wiley was thinking to himself, this is right, thank you God.

He had hooked four folding chairs to the back of the jeep, two blankets and a pillow.

"The pillow will make it easier for you to sit, and one blanket will keep the chill off you, while the boys lounge around on the second one." Wiley told her.

She flashed a big smile back. Both boys were smiling in the back seat too; they weren't used to anyone doing something kind for them, even such a small thing as a blanket to sit on. The boys were feeling very safe; anyone would be an idiot to harass them with this big dude looking after them.

When they pulled into the amphitheater parking space, both boys jumped out and unhooked the chairs, each grabbing two. They saw a spot they wanted so they ran to grab it before anyone else could. Wiley helped Annabelle out of the jeep, picked up the pillow and blankets and headed after the boys.

"Ahhh," Wiley was saying to himself, "our first public family outing."

Deputy Homer was on duty before eight. He would be walking down one side of the 'square', and Special Deputy Sonny would be canvassing the other side. That way one of them would be only a breath away in the event of a problem. Special Deputy Sonny had a badge pinned on his shirt, and his buttons were almost busting; he had said the Oath of upholding the law. He was one proud Special Deputy. Todd was noting his demure.

Woods People were coming out of every where carrying blankets, paper and plastic sacks of goods, along with furniture and plants. The square was rapidly becoming bustling and noisy. The band was in full swing now, and dancers were congregating on the dance floor. Most of the songs were slower for right now. The square dance callers wouldn't be starting until about one o'clock. Todd was hoping Cecil and Lloyd would remember to keep their progressive dances low key so kids could enjoy them too. These dances were not for competition today, just strictly fun.

Clarence Bloom sat down at the piano to spare Kelli, and Will was blowing his harmonica, and his violin was sitting safely under the piano. Todd took Kelli's hand and walked her to the dance floor. He took her loosely into his arms as they started dancing. They would keep catching each other's eyes, and sparks would ignite a big smile that spread out on each of their faces. Both seemed sad when the song ended, and he kissed her on the end of her nose. The two started back toward the band, hand in hand.

Pam took a Mic and started singing 'When Irish Eyes Are Smilin' and the Special Deputy froze. Sonny didn't know she sang like a meadowlark. He didn't leave his post; in fact, he didn't even remember he had a post as his eyes were fixated on her.

Todd was watching, and started to smile. Kelli asked him what he was smiling at, and he said, "Looks like we have two Homers." She nodded.

"By the time Jani gets here, we'll be almost without police protection." Todd chuckled at her.

Jake's ATV pulled into Angela's. Here she came, right on target, and he was waiting for her. He missed her too, and was anxiously waiting the time when they didn't have to part at each day's end. He held her so close and long, first kissing her forehead, then her nose, and then her waiting sweet lips.

"How's my beautiful lady today?" He asked the little red head cuddled into him, being careful to not bump his cast.

"I'm fin' now." Her soft little voice purrrred. She must have blown just a bit into his ear because the big man shivered.

They got Orpha all situated in the ATV. Angela had brought her mother a jacket and two extra blankets. She threw them in the rumble seat as she, Mike, along with his trumpet, and Carrie jumped in the back, squeezing to fit together. Angela had managed to get the spot right behind her man, and was hanging on.

When the ATV reached the amphitheater and parked, Jake started to pick up Orpha, but a voice came from behind him saying. "I'll get her." Billy Carson was reaching for Orpha as Mike stepped up to help. Billy had brought a lounge chair with him, and had it already set up by the dance floor with a couple of blankets in the bottom of it to sit on. He had screwed an eighteen-inch hook to the side of it for her bag. Orpha's arm was in full swing as the music reached her ears. The two young men sat her down and Jake put the blanket over her as Angela fixed the bag on the hook. Orpha had her own entourage.

"We'll take first watch." Billy said to Jake as he sat down beside Orpha. Carrie sat down on the opposite side.

Jake took his love's hand and the two of them walked onto the dance floor. As they moved across the floor, it was as though there was no one else in the entire park. Her hand seemed to be automatically holding up her ring finger so everyone could see she and Jake were engaged. He couldn't hold her too close and create a bad impression with the youngun's, but just to have her within touching distance was good enough for now.

Jake and Angela took a break to check on Orpha. As they walked up, Billy asked Carrie if she would like to dance.

"Yes." Carrie replied and the two headed for the dance floor. The band was still doing fairly slow dances. Billy was careful not to take any liberties or advances with her; he knew she is only seventeen.

As the big man and his little red head sat there talking to Orpha and singing to her with the band, Deputy Homer sauntered up very slowly. Jake could tell he had something to say to him, but he thought he'd just let the scenario play out in Homer's timing.

"Mr. Jake," the deputy finally had enough guts to say, "would it be all right, I mean would you care - I mean if I promise to be good, I mean - if I keep remembering she is only seventeen, would it be possible - would you let me - can I have your permission to ask Jani to dance?"

He finally got the jumbled up sentence spit out. Jake was cracking up inside, giving Homer all the time he needed to complete his proposition. The young deputy stood waiting for Jake's answer.

Angela finally poked Jake to quit tormenting Homer.

"Sure." The big man finally agreed.

Homer was waiting for a bunch of orders but none came. He stood there waiting for Jake to say something else, but Jake put his attention back on Orpha. Homer still stood there a few more moments, and then went back to his patrolling.

Jess was taking the long way to the amphitheater. He was savoring this beautiful lady riding with him, the wind blowing through their hair, and how good she smelled. He could have rode around all day, but he knew that darned ATV would come looking for them.

"Have you ever danced, Beth?" Jess asked her.

"No." She answered.

"OK, well you're going to get a chance, because I will be taking you out on the dance floor. We'll just do slow ones until you get the hang of it." Jess informed and assured her, as he pulled into a parking spot and shut the car off. Beth waited for Jess to come around and get her door; Emily was rubbing off on her. She is a lady.

Jess kept noticing, however, that in the middle of a conversation she would suddenly stare off as something would grip her thoughts, and her aura would become despondent and often her eyes would fill with tears. He could usually bring her back with an 'earth to Beth'. When the time is right, he will ask her what's going on in her pretty head that makes her so sad.

Ernie Caldwell and his son Alex had shown up on the scene. Tom Lacey had brought the Paramedic truck with him in case of an emergency. So Alex went over to check in with him. Ernie's wife, Eva, was minding the eatery along with Elaine, and he would spell them later. It's hard for the two of them to get away at the same time. Eva and Ernie are actually hoping their twenty-three year old son Alex, or fifteen-year old daughter Elaine will eventually get interested in restaurant management.

Alex does serve as a cook sometimes, but his heart is not really into food, other than to eat it. They know their son is very satisfied where he is, and they know he is doing a good thing. Alex had gone to City Hospital right out of high school and taken some courses there for Paramedic training, and he has learned a lot from Tom Lacey.

Elaine can't seem to keep her eyes off the fellas long enough to learn much about the eatery, although she does wait tables now. And when Lexie Lacey drops in – the two get the giggles, and work stops on their end. Plus the girls have hollow legs where soda is concerned.

Tom has been a Paramedic for about fifteen years; he seems to know as much as most doctors do. He and his wife, Lois, have four kids ranging from fifteen to twenty-two years old. Their twenty one-year old son, Tom Junior, went into the Air Force right out of high school. That's probably where Mike Crabtree got the idea to join the service. Tom Jr. has been home a few times in his striking uniform, and Mike knows he gets paid well.

The band started playing "Be My Love". And as Will Armstrong started playing his violin softly, Wiley took Annabelle's hand and asked her to dance.

"I don't know how." She stated.

"That's OK, I'll lead you. You'll be just fine." He answered as he kept a hold of her hand.

She stood up, and the two of them walked hand in hand onto the dance floor. Wiley was careful not to be too precocious and scare her. But as he led her around the floor, it felt right. And, when their eyes would meet and she would smile, there went his heart again, pitter pat, pitter pat. Wiley would have been happy with an ugly wife, but God was giving him a truly beautiful woman instead, and she would make his biggest dream come true – being a father.

Wayne and Wilson were over looking at the ostrich Barstow had brought to town in the large open topped horse trailer. He had taken the big bird out of the trailer and the ostrich was securely tied to the trailer to keep it from taking off. The trailer was securely hitched to his red truck; that aggressive and foul fowl wouldn't take off with that much weight. The kids were going crazy trying to talk to the ostrich Barstow called Stickers. Stickers got his name – not from sticky fingers, but from a sticky beak. He was always stealing things.

In just the short time he had been there at the Exchange, Stickers had already gotten one hat, a kids bag of popcorn and a ladies pocket book – that Barstow had to retrieve amid giggles.

Barstow was noting Wiley had Annabelle on the dance floor. He could also see both boys glancing often over their way, and he was trying to figure out the expressions on the boy's faces. Wiley was keeping things respectful, he had said he would. Barstow also saw Annabelle keep smiling. He knew she hadn't had any smiles for many years. Perhaps Wiley was right, God is putting this family together – but he was still concerned about the boy's reactions.

Keep it slow Wiley. Barstow thought to himself.

Shoppers scurried all over the place, holding up garments for size and condition. Lamps and shades were walking off; old jewelry was being tried on. The popcorn stand and the sno-cone trailer were overflowing with customers. Cans of soda lay chilling in big tubs filled with ice. The town didn't allow alcoholic drinks to be sold at the Exchange because of the bad influence on the kids. But the 'Jumpin' Pub' was just across the street for anyone who wanted to have a drink.

Pam was sitting in the shade on a concrete step right stage of the amphitheater journalizing everything she could see.

Sonny walked up to her as he said, "Todd said I could ask you to dance, and that's a mighty pretty song playing now. Will you have this dance with me?"

Pam was listening to "Silvery Moon" as she answered, "That is a very pretty song, and yes, I'd like to dance with you Sonny."

She had said his name, he heard her say his name – wow. He held his hand out, she took it and stood up, and they walked onto the dance floor. She is about six inches shorter than he is so he could see Todd watching him right over her head. But it didn't matter; he was planning on being a gentleman with this lady.

She even polished the fingerprints off his badge as they danced. He felt she might be a bit proud of him doing something right.

It seemed they were both sad when the song ended, but he asked her if she would dance with him again after he checked his 'post', and she said yes. When she went back and sat down on the step and started writing again, he wondered if she was writing about him. And if so, what?

Jake and Angela were back on the dance floor when the little pink bug drove in. Several of the young foxes started her way. Jani was still a bit freaked from her attempted rape experience, so the big man guided his lady toward the end of the dance floor to keep the little Volkswagen in sight.

Then Jake saw Homer focused on Jani. She shut the car off, and walked around to her trunk. Homer picked up her lawn chair, blanket and cooler. Then he led her over to where Orpha was sitting. He unfolded her chair and placed her blanket in it. Perhaps Homer was remembering the horror Jani had gone through, and that's why he wanted her right where Jake could see her…And himself. Jake wasn't sure the young man had even said a word to her…maybe he couldn't speak right now. But he seemed to quietly take the upper hand. With the Deputy and Jake looking after her, the foxes backed off.

Soon, Homer and Sonny were back in their routine, which is as much of a routine as two lovesick pups could be in.

The deputy went back to where Jani was sitting. "Miss Jani," Homer stammered, "I asked yur brother for permission, I mean, it's ok with him, I mean it'll be all right if we dance."

"I'd like to." Jani answered without any wavering in her voice.

Homer wasn't sure what to do next – should he touch her? He started to put his hand out to Jani, and then pulled it back. How should he touch her? Should he take her arm – or her hand – or just point to the dance floor?

Jani watched him curiously for a couple of minutes, and then she reached for his hand and said, "Let's go."

With the touch of her hand, Homer could hardly stand up, is knees became jelly. It felt so strange. He's always dreamed of touching her hand, but he didn't think he would go to jelly. *I need to get myself together.* Homer scolded himself.

Jani led the way as they moved over to the dance floor. "Do you know how to dance?" She asked the shivering young man.

"I've been looking at it on the computer," the deputy confessed, "but I don't know much about dancing."

Jani was getting tickled, as she caught the young deputy's eyes. She could tell he was mesmerized. He kept stumbling.

Finally she said, "We'll go over to the edge where not too many can see us and practice."

"Jake will still be able to see us won't he?" Homer asked.

"Sure will." She answered as she caught Jake's twinkling eyes.

Jani had a hard time getting Homer to even put his arm part way around her waist. She put it there for him, and then put her hand in his. She could see he was completely in la la land. They 'danced at' dancing for a while. Then she reached up and felt Homer's arm and shoulder muscles.

"Wow, you're really filling out Homer…looking good!" She grinned at him.

He was too embarrassed to say anything, so he just looked into her eyes as he blushed.

 Finally she said, "I'm thirsty, let's get a soda."

He obligingly agreed. Homer was a bit irritated with himself for being such a dork – but he just couldn't help it – he was so infatuated with Jani, he was worthless. They got sodas and he walked her back over to Jake who had a silly grin parting his lips.

"May I come back later, Miss Jani, after I check my patrol?" Homer asked her.

"Sure, that would be nice Homer." She answered.

Angela giggled and hugged Jake as she whispered in his ear, "Good thin' ya' hav' four sets o eyes an' ears with all th' young wooin' aroun' here."

Jake shivered again at Angela's breath in his ear as he agreed.

Up pulled Ira's old red Dodge pickup. It had been washed and waxed; Jake figured the old truck was in shock. Ira took a lounge chair out of the back and set it up by Jake's chair, and went back to the truck. Moments later here he came carrying Leslie.

"Thought some fresh air might be good for her," he told Jake, "she's been cooped up for a few days now."

Leslie thought he was going to put her down in the chair, as she leaned over toward it, but he just adjusted her in his arms and headed for the dance floor. He started dancing to the music, swinging his load all around and they were both laughing their heads off.

"Don't you drop me." She warned him.

"Not a chance." Ira assured her.

The GMC pulled in, and much to everyone's surprise, out stepped John Judd and Josie. How did he get her out of the mountain? Jani told her mom she didn't know she was coming, but Angela had called and said quite a show is being played out, and she didn't want Mam to miss anything.

"Besides," Josie added, "all my family's here."

Emily moved their chairs over by the Judd gang too. It was

a real family gathering. Mia was helping Barstow corral Stickers, and keep the kids a safe distance from him. John Stoddard had brought two pairs of pull horses hitched to a hayrack, and was giving everyone free rides. The horses even seemed to be enjoying the festivities, and especially the treats people were feeding them.

Jess and Beth hadn't done much dancing. They had gotten sodas and popcorn and were sitting on a bench by themselves – but within Jake's view. It looked like they were in some pretty serious conversation when her grandpa Roscoe walked up. Jess scooted over, so did Beth, closer to Jess, so Roscoe would have room to join them. It seemed like Jess and Roscoe took over the conversation and Beth was just listening to them. Jake wasn't sure what all the deep talk was about, but something was troubling his spirit.

The big man came back to reality as Homer was saying to Jani, "Miss Jani, we can go for a hayrack ride, would you like that? With Mr. Jake's permission of course." Homer looked over at Jake and the big brother nodded his approval.

Mam was watching the young man trying to be cool this time – Angela had told her about his first attempt at talking to Jani. She put her hand out, and he nervously took it and the two headed for the horses and the wagon full of hay bales.

About that time Cecil and Lloyd showed up ready for square dancing.

"Let's pick your partners," Cecil said into the Mic, "we need four couples for each square."

Eight couples showed up so they could have two squares.

While everyone was getting set up for the squares, Todd and Kelli ran over to the Soda tubs for quick pick-me-ups. As he put his hand in the ice, she reached down and held it under the water's edge. He acted like she had him held down solidly, but he suddenly brought his hand up out of the water filled with ice cubes. He gave her a sheepish grin and she took off, with him right after her. She knew what he was intending to do with that freezing ice.

By then everyone was watching as he chased her up around the amphitheater, through the musicians, and back behind the piano. She was caught, no escape. But instead of dropping the ice down her back, he threw it over at Will, who sadly just let it drop to the ground. He didn't want to tangle with his sister.

The four couples in each group were now in their places, and the music had started. Lloyd would be calling the first dance, starting with the basic movements, to get everyone in the mood for the faster swings, dos-a-dos, free spins and grape vines. Each one of the 'sets' had a teen couple in them to learn how to dance. The music played faster and faster as the couples did lots of Reverse Turns, Allemande Lefts and Twirls. The head couples were laughing at the side couples that included the two young couples as mistakes were being made. There was slipping and sliding into each other – and it was all in good fun.

As Jani started to scale the hayrack, Homer finally got up enough courage to take her arm and stabilize her as she climbed on it. Then he jumped up on the rack after her. By this time Jake had quit worrying about Jani, it was obvious she was safe. Homer kept a hold of Jani's arm until she got seated on a bale of hay, and he knew she wasn't going to fall. As the rack started moving, he casually put his arm around her waist to keep her from falling off the hayrack like he'd seen a kid do once. He liked the way she looked right now – she didn't need any remodeling. Her safety had made him step up to the plate this time.

Jake and Angela, Todd and Kelli, Billy and Carrie – and Ira and Leslie, got into the next set of squares. Cecil would be calling this dance.

Wiley had convinced Annabelle and the boys to get in to the second square. The boys are brothers and could be partners, nothing wrong with that – and no one would dare say there is. Annabelle and the boys had been watching the first 'sets', so they now had some idea of what to do. Yes Sir, Wiley's little family was having fun.

Everyone kept asking Orpha if she was tired, but she kept relating no by her movements. Jake kept telling her he would take her home any time she wanted to go, but her eyes kept saying no.

Josie was getting a chance to talk to Orpha; she was talking about the soon to be wedding of Orpha's daughter and her son. Josie didn't even act like Orpha might not be able to understand her, and talked to her normally. She told her that the four girls were going to go to the City for wedding clothes, and that included getting Orpha a new dress. Mam said she didn't know what colors the two lovebirds wanted yet, but she'd find out, and get her a dress to match the wedding colors. Orpha kept watching Josie's face, and her eyes were smiling and saying I understand.

When the hayrack got back to the starting point, Homer jumped off and told Jani to just sit down on the side of the rack. When she did he reached up and took hold of her waist and helped her jump down. He seemed stronger than Jani had imagined. Jani was five-feet-six inches, so she imagined him about five-feet-ten inches, she was glad he was taller than she was.

Sonny came over and asked Homer if it would be all right for him to take a break and take Pam for a hayride, and Homer said sure. Pam wasn't singing with the square dance music, so when Sonny invited her she agreed.

Sonny had watched Homer help Jani up on the hayrack so he mimicked Homer and took Pam's arm to stabilize her. Then he put his arm around her waist to keep her from falling off – just like a real man.

Ira and Leslie were a hoot doing the square dances; everyone was laughing so hard they could hardly move. Even Cecil was cracking up as he was doing the calls.

Annabelle got with the program really fast, and after their embarrassment got over at dancing with their brother, the two boys were having a good time too.

The entire day was wonderful; everyone had a complete ball. Angela, Josie, Jani and Kelli were talking about their trip to the City in the morning for a wedding gown.

"Meet me at the corner about eight o'clock." Jani told Angela and Kelli.

As Jake took Orpha home, his little red head was hanging onto his neck from the rumble seat again. He helped Angela get her mother into bed; they knew she would be sleeping through the night now. She looked very tired. Todd was bringing Kelli, Carrie, Mike, Will and Pam home after bit.

"That little Toyota will be a groaning, and it will really be togetherness," Jake mused, "and Kelli will be forced to sit close to Todd."

Jake really didn't want them to rush getting home; he wanted some time alone with his lady. As they sat in Angela's living room, and he took her in his arms she blew into his ear again.

The big man shivered as he said to her, "Where'd you learn to do that?"

He realized the times before hadn't been an accident; she had made him shiver intentionally.

"Girls jus' know." She answered him as she did it again.

"You stop that," he told her firmly, "it hard enough to behave around you without you doing that."

She planted a long kiss on his lips; he could almost feel her lips parting, and then back up to catch his eyes as she grinned at him. He knew she was having a hard time controlling herself too. As their lips met again, and they clutched each other tightly, he knew he had to work even faster on completing his project. Had to get a hold of Ira first thing in the morning, and have him bring Todd with him. Nature was really trying to take control. He loves this woman so much it almost hurts, and leaving her is getting impossible, and he knows she feels the same way.

It's probably a good thing they were interrupted by Todd's car doors.

Sheriff Leo had been conspicuously absent at the Exchange.

Wedding Shopping

Eight o'clock sharp, Angela and Kelli were at the corner waiting when the little pink bug showed up. Jani was driving, and Mam was in the rider seat. Josie got out so the two girls could get into the back seat.

"You ladies had breakfast?" Mam asked.

"Yea," Angela answered softly, "I had one of Jake's energy bars he left for me and Kelli had one too."

Mam grinned.

Chatter was high as the little bug curved around and down the winding mountain road. Mam had made a 'potential list' to share with Jake's little red head; she didn't know how much Angela had planned.

"What are yours and Jake's colors?" Josie asked.

"Well," Angela responded, "Jake and I like green and white. Does that soun' ok?"

"Sounds really beautiful, Honey, what about the flowers?" Mam continued.

"Well, roses arn't green, but they can mak' carnations green by puttin, somethin' in the water, so we thought white roses an' green carnations." Angela answered.

"Wow," Jani cut in, "white roses and green carnations sounds gorgeous, and maybe some baby's breath put in for a filler?"

Angela liked the idea of baby's breath – so did grandma-to-be.

By the time they drove the two hours to the City, everyone was hungry. Mam had noticed Kelli being quiet and deep in thought.

"You all right Kelli?" Mam asked her as Jani pulled into The Sweet Dragon.

"Yea, I'm jus' thinkin'" Kelli said gazingly.

Mam could tell the sparks in her eyes wasn't from anything she had said.

"She's thinkin' of Todd," honest little Angela blurted out, "she's gettin' it bad, she's been sweet on him since grade school. We used to walk by 'is house so she might see 'em."

"Does Todd know how you feel?" Mam asked.

"Nope, I don't know if he likes me too," Kelli confessed, "and I don't want to embarrass him or me."

"Well, at the wedding with you all dressed up so pretty, maybe he'll give you a clue Kelli." Mam suggested.

"I hope so, Mam." The young lady remarked.

After lunch the ladies headed for a bridal shop called 'Bridal Boutique', the windows were all decorated with beautiful bridal and maidens dresses. Angela was getting so excited she was giddy.   As they stepped into the shop, the owner Zoe Bright came over to them as ask if she could help them.

The cat seemed to have gotten Angela's tongue, so Jani answered for her, "Yes, we're looking for a nice wedding gown for my new sister-in-law."

"Can she wear white?" Zoe asked.

"Sure can," Jani responded, "she's pure."

"We're also looking for a bride maid's gown, a green one." Jani continued.

"What color of green?" Zoe inquired.

"An emerald green one," Angela chimed in, 'made of satin and velvet."

Zoe took all of both Angela and Kelli's measurements. Zoe was right, Kelli's dress had to be special ordered, and it would take about three weeks.

"That's ok," Angela told Zoe, "long as it's not longer."

Now Mam had an idea of when the wedding would be – shortly after three weeks.

Jani kept picking out gowns for Angela to try on and model. The little red head was breathtaking in every one of the beautiful white gowns. Mam even lost her breath a couple of times. She tried on fourteen gowns, then one with beads strung all across the back and over the shoulders. It had a train that went behind her about six feet, and a loop that fit over her wrist to keep the train off the floor when they were dancing. The same beads veiled across the front and around the waist, and at the bottom where the edge was scalloped up in small Austrian looking bows. All three of the ladies were silent as they looked at her – she was beyond beautiful. Mam's eyes filled with tears – this is Jake's wife – and the mother of my grandchildren, and she is an angel.

Angela asked Zoe if she had a hairpiece to match the gown, and she did. As Angela slipped it on her head and pulled the netting down over her face, she really looked like a bride. The headpiece also had the same beads streaming down the side and back of the piece, and everything was attached to a tiara full of crystals and beads.

Zoe also had lace gloves to match, without fingers. Angela had never seen gloves without fingers, and thought they were funny. But she liked them because you could still see her engagement ring, and Jake could put her wedding ring on all right too. The waist would have to be taken in about an inch, but that was no problem, it could be done within the week.

Shoes were next; Mam suggested she get some that are really comfortable, because she would be standing for quite a while. They picked out a long slip and white lace panty hose. Then came the garter.

"What's that for?" Angela asked Zoe.

"You wear it on your leg, and your husband takes it off with his teeth and throws it to the next groom, supposedly. Just like you throw your bouquet to the next bride." Zoe informed her.

As Zoe said how Jake takes it off her leg, Angela turned bright read, and got so flustered she couldn't speak.

"We'll take it." Jani piped up, as she grinned at her mom.

Jani helped Zoe and Kelli finish designing Kelli's gown.

"We want some of the same kind of beads that are on Angela's wedding gown," Jani was informing Zoe, who didn't have a problem with the beads at all.

"They'll be white." Zoe told Jani.

"That's perfect." Jani responded.

They did have slipper satin low heels for the ladies to wear that had lots of foam inside of them.

"These are the most comfortable shoes we have, you can wear these all day and your feet won't hurt. They're a bit expensive, but their worth the extra money. The beads can also be put on the bride's shoes to match her gown, and an emerald bow can be made to match Kelli's dress. Sound all right?" Zoe asked Angela, who looked over at Mam for an up or down nod.

"Absolutely, they're perfect." Mam answered.

Zoe also fitted Kelli with a long black underskirt, which was already in stock. Both Angela's and Kelli's underskirts would go home with them today, and Angela's headpiece. Kelli would wear white lace panty hose too. Zoe brought out a smaller tiara she said could be made up to match the emerald gown. Kelli was thrilled.

Now for the mother's dresses.

"What colors would you like for us mother's to wear, Honey?" Mam asked Angela.

"Jake an' I like pink, or yellow, or blue, just what you like." Jakes little red head told her.

Zoe bought out the measuring tape and said that perhaps she should get her measurements – then see what she had in stock.

"Well, looks like a size six should work." Zoe stated as she started thumbing through the rack, and showing various dresses to Mam and Angela. Jani and Kelli were looking through dresses to fit Jani, who wanted a green print if they could find one in her size.

Yea," Kelli agreed, "green will go with your eyes."

They also had the task of finding a nice dress that would fit Orpha, one that could have Velcro put up and down the back of it so it would slip on the front of her easily and be closed in the back. Angela had measured her feet, and even though she wouldn't be walking the shoes should match her dress. They found a pretty mint green print rayon dress, and Zoe said she could have it altered to have the open back with Velcro. The rayon would be cool and light. Mam was afraid a zipper might scratch Orpha. Jani found some really cute satin slippers that had the mint green in them, and a small handbag to match. Mam found a small feather barrette that had mint; blue, gold and violet feathers that would be perfect for Orpha's hair, now she would look finished too.

Jake would be getting the flowers and corsages. Mam snickered a bit, wondering what her son would pick out. He just needed the colors of everyone's gowns and dresses first to match them.

Mam found her a very sheik and tailored looking two piece suit. It was a powder blue with multicolored sequins on the front of the jacket forming butterflies and a rope belt across the back. It was about calf length. When she came out to model it, everyone clapped – it was a winner.

"Mam," Jani said to her, "you're not supposed to look prettier than the bride."

Her daughter's kind remarks made Mam feel good. Zoe found some powder blue shoes with sequins on them, with a matching purse. Josie also needed a new slip and a headpiece. She picked out a large comb with tiny white and blue roses, and crystals on it.

"Perfect." Josie whispered.

They were in the store for over four hours.   But it looked like most everything was covered. Jake had given Angela some money to help pay for things, but Mam wouldn't take any money from her.

"Dad and I are going to pay for the clothes, Honey," Mam told her, "you and Jake can take care of the flowers and renting the tuxes."

Angela gave her new mom a hug, and a great big thank you. Kelli also gave Mam a big hug and thank you. Jani joined in the celebration, and soon everyone was hugging everyone else, even Zoe.

It had been an absolutely marvelous day. Everyone seemed tired as the little pink bug started back toward Raincroft, after going through the McDonald's drive through for coffee and snacks to keep everyone awake.

The only thing Angela was sad about was that her father, Manny, wouldn't be at her wedding and give her away. Her brother Mike will do the honors. Jess will be Best Man, and Will and Little Joe will be ushers. Carrie Crabtree will play the piano, and she and

Todd will sing. Of course, John Stoddard will be performing the ceremony.

Billy will make two trips with Jake's ATV. The first to bring Angela, Kelli and Carrie to church, the second to get Orpha with Pam's help. They also had to get Orpha's wheel chair. Todd would get all the clothes to church the day before. Dad and Josie would pick up all the flowers early in the morning in the GMC along with the punch.

Mam was really excited. Everything was almost ready, but she still didn't know the date yet. She knew Jake was almost finished with the apartment, and all the furniture was in place. She hadn't seen him carrying in any food yet.

Mobile Home Shopping

Wiley picked up Annabelle and the boys about nine o'clock. The boys were in the Jeep before he could even get the vehicle shut off.

"What's the surprise?" They were begging their driver.

"Now, if I told you, it wouldn't be a surprise – would it?" Wiley answered them.

Their lips puckered with disappointment, but they guessed they'd just have to wait.

Wiley was up on the porch as Annabelle stepped out the door. Wiley smiled at her as he told her, "You are prettier than any picture."

He took her arm to be sure she didn't fall through the steps as she answered him, "Thank you Wiley."

He opened the jeep door for her and helped her in – so she wouldn't fall – then shut the door.

"We'll be taking a trip to the City. Got something to look at." Wiley told his captive audience.

As his eyes met Annabelle's, the sparks flew again, from both of their eyes. He knew in his heart of hearts that she was responding positively to him, and there goes his heart again, pitter-pat, pitter-pat. Good thing he's got a strong heart, he allowed, a weak one might burst. He was truly enthralled at what a beautiful little lady she is.

Thank you so much Lord for giving me a beautiful wife. He was praying and thanking the Lord in his thoughts.

As they got to the edge of the City, Wiley asked the family "Is anyone hungry yet?"

"Yes." Came two voices from the back seats.

Of course, the big man thought to himself, *they have hollow legs.*

Wiley pulled into The Sweet Dragon; here the boys could eat all they want, including desserts. He carried Annabelle's plate as she loaded it with things she likes, and he was making note. After he got her and the boys settled at a table, Wiley said grace. Then he went back and filled his plate. Most of the things Annabelle liked were his favorites too.

"Yep," he said to himself, "we certainly go together."

Back in the Jeep and on the road again, but this time not too far. To everyone's surprise, Wiley pulled into a Mobile Home Dealership called 'United Homes'.

Pretty apropos. Wiley thought to himself.

"What's this?" Annabelle asked.

"Well, we need to pick you out a new home, and I thought the boys should help since they will be living there too." He answered her.

"Wow!" Joyous voices were coming from the back; "can we go and look in them?"

"Absolutely, you're going to be buying one, so look at them all and see what you like and don't like." Wiley called after them.

He opened Annabelle's door and took her hand to help her out. "Let's see what you like and don't." Wiley said to the smiling lady.

They walked through the first home.

"I never thought I'd have something like this Wiley." She said to the big man.

"You deserve the best, Annabelle." He answered, as he held her arm down the first set of steps.

Here came a salesman saying, "Those your kids? They can't be going through all these homes; we have to keep them clean for buyers."

Annabelle could feel Wiley bristle as he answered, "Yea, those are our boys, and they can look at every home here a dozen times if they want to. They are paying customers; in fact they are cash customers. If you don't want our boys to pick out their home, we can sure go somewhere else."

Annabelle and the boys were overwhelmed at Wiley's sticking up for the boys. For years she had to be the protector of the family, Wayne Sr. had been so frail he couldn't do anything for them. He had been bedridden for years, and she had to carry the entire load. It felt so good for someone to help bear her cross, and her boy's. *This booming voice is a really good man and he cares, he really cares.* She thought to herself.

Annabelle was thinking that he has made no improper advances toward her the last few weeks they have been spending together. She could feel the sparks when their eyes met, and she wondered if he could.

They looked through home after home. It was fun. Annabelle would pick things out she liked and some that she didn't. She really liked the split floor plan homes, the bedrooms were a lot more private, and each master suite had its own bath. She found one doublewide she really loved, and so did the boys. In fact, when the boys first stepped into the home they were emotionally moving into it already, they had even picked which bedroom they wanted without squabble. Annabelle looked into every cabinet, drawer, appliance, oven, dishwasher and nook. They all sat on the sofa, in the chairs and looked out the windows. Annabelle reached over and squeezed Wiley's hand. It told him this was her choice.

"This is your mom's choice, Boys," he said to them, "what do you think, can you get along with this home?"

A resounding 'yes' came from both of them.

"So be it." Wiley affirmed as the boys darted off to their very own bedrooms to lie down on their very own new beds.

The salesman came in as he said, "Looks like this is the one your family wants, how much will you be putting down and what kind of monthly payments are you looking for?"

Annabelle still had a hold of Wiley's hand as he continued talking to the salesman, "We won't be needing financing, make up a cash sale, including delivery, set up, and all the existing furniture. I'll let you know how soon to deliver it, probably about five or six weeks yet; we're still working on the land. And, on the Bill of Sale,

I want you to list all the furniture as going with the home for the sale price, along with complete delivery and set up. There will be a stem wall; about eighteen inches above ground so the floors stay dry and warmer. I need the 'specs' for the home to finish the preparation and layout."

Annabelle's heart was pounding with pride, both for the gorgeous new home, and for this man's heart of gold caring for her and her boys. She never in her wildest dreams thought she would ever have a home like this, it's right out of a movie, furniture and all. There were even double doors on the master bedroom and a walk-in closet that is larger than her living room at the trailer. The big tub in the bathroom even had holes all around the sides. She had pointed to them and Wiley told her the tub is a Jacuzzi, that it will massage her and help her to relax. Everything in the bathroom was ceramic, including the two sinks. She had never seen chandeliers over a bathroom sink, but there were three of them. A small closet was just inside the front door for guests to put their coats in.

The boy's bathroom also had two sinks with chandeliers over them, and they had already picked out whose was whose. The floral sofa and chair were the most comfortable she had ever sat on, and the fabric matched the drapes. She was amazed that she would have two matching lamps and even a coffee table that matched the two end tables the lamps were sitting on. There was an icemaker in the refrigerator, and you could push a bar on the outside and ice would spit out at you. By pressing a button above the water and ice dispenser, you could choose either cubes or crushed that you could pour soda over. Or you could get just plain cold water with another button.

The salesman asked them to step into the office with him. The boys wanted to wait for them in their new home, and Wiley told them sure. Annabelle still had a hold of Wiley's hand as they walked toward the office.

"I'll write them a check for the total, so you won't ever have to worry about house payments." He told her.

After the paperwork was done and the bank funds had been verified, Wiley told the salesman to give the lady a key to her new home. He hesitated because they usually don't give keys until a home is delivered to its owner's lot. But with the home paid for, and Wiley's firm expression, he handed a key to Annabelle and told her congratulations. She was squeezing Wiley's hand really good now, he could see her delight, and that delighted him.

The family was really excited and chatty when they started for home. But before too long, the boys both conked out. It had been a big day for them and the wind hitting their faces them made them sleepy. The booming voice pulled over to the side of the road and draped a blanket across both boys so they wouldn't get chilled with their inactivity.

"Wiley," Annabelle whispered, "I don' know what ta say, thans is not enuf. I didn't know the meeting at church had raised money to pay for all this," then she paused before she continued, "it didn't, did it? You paid for our new home, didn't you Wiley?"

Wiley took a deep breath before he answered her point blank question honestly, "Yes Annabelle, the money taken in at the church will go into the boy's school fund, or possibly medical bills. I didn't want you to know about me paying for the home, because I don't want you to be beholding to me. I want us to just be us and not because of anything monetary."

Annabelle took his hand again and squeezed it, and Wiley gently squeezed back, his heart was still praising God for his blessings.

Pitter-Pat – Pitter-Pat   ☺

Author's Bio

Mystery Mountain Two is the second in the series of Raincroft California Mountain living. It is the author's third published works.

Marie Grace loves the mountains, and escapes to them for a few days as often as time and circumstances will allow. Her favorite color is emerald green, so she naturally enjoys evergreen trees.

Her love for animals is evident all through her writings, and she sincerely hopes her love for the critters will rub off on her readers. She had an apricot Toy Poodle for about fifteen years named Missey Sue Elizabeth Mutley. Missey actually called Marie "Mama." The first time her oldest nephew, Jerry, heard her he could hardly believe his ears and he called his Aunt Marie to verify what he thought he heard. It was true and clear.

The author's love for Jesus is the most important thing in her life, and she also hopes you will pick up some of that love from all three of her books, *Thoughts Aplenty, Mystery Mountain* and *Mystery Mountain Two.*

Thank you.

www.ingramcontent.com/pod-product-compliance
Lightning Source LLC
Chambersburg PA
CBHW051701180726
48283CB00004B/1170